Double Buckeyes

A Story of the Way America Used To Be

By

Bud Shuster

 WHITE MANE BOOKS

This White Mane Books publication
was printed by
Beidel Printing House, Inc.
63 West Burd Street
Shippensburg, PA 17257-0152 USA

In respect for the scholarship contained herein, the acid-free paper used in this book meets the guidelines for permanence and durability of the Committee on Production Guidelines for Book Longevity of the Council on Library Resources.

For a complete list of available publications
please write
White Mane Books
Division of White Mane Publishing Company, Inc.
P.O. Box 152
Shippensburg, PA 17257-0152 USA

Library of Congress Cataloging-in-Publication Data

Shuster, Bud.
    Double Buckeyes : a story of the way America used to be / by Bud Shuster.
        p.   cm.
    Summary: In western Pennsylvania during World War II, eleven-year-old Little Buck makes a shocking discovery when his beloved grandfather dies, causing him to question his very identity.
    ISBN 1-57249-176-0 (alk. paper). -- ISBN 1-57249-177-9 (softcover : alk. paper)
    [1. Grandfathers Fiction. 2. Family Fiction. 3. Pennsylvania Fiction.] I. Title.
PZ7.S559855Do   1999
[Fic]--dc21   99-35560
                                                                   CIP

To

My wife, Patricia, and our loved ones of yesteryear, who sacrificed so we might thrive.

Contents

v

Introduction

Set in a small town in the steel valley of western Pennsylvania amid the Great Depression and World War II, *Double Buckeyes* is the touching story of a boy's love for his grandfather and the shocking discovery that nearly breaks his heart. It is about a family's struggles through hard and dangerous times, and the profound impact early experiences can have on a young child's life. It is a reminder that love can survive death, and it is indestructible despite terrible challenges.

Chapter One

Searching

Crawling on his hands and knees in the ivy beneath the buckeye tree, the eleven-year-old lad seemed to be frantically searching for something. Tears streamed down his sunburnt cheeks as he rooted through the thick green foliage, feeling for what apparently was not there. Tossing his head back, he tried unsuccessfully to flick his fine blond hair out of his blue eyes. It was as soft as baby corn silk. He then ran a dirty hand through his hair, smudging his forehead.

Glancing at the big white house behind him, he saw his mother and grandmother watching him through the picture window, his mother waving, smiling forlornly as if her heart would break, while his grandmother stared austerely through him.

Waving at his mother, he continued his fruitless search for another few minutes, and then rose, brushing the dirt off his corduroy knickers and pulling up his long brown stockings to just below his knees. He hated long stockings, and knickers even more. But that was what his grandmother, Nan, had said he should wear, and his mother had given in. He had complained to his father, but because he was away, except on weekends, working in the war effort against Hitler, his father had shrugged it off, saying, "Best you do like they say."

Big Buck, his grandfather, had tousled his hair and winked, "Just don't let any of your buddies know that those knickers give you an edge against them in their long pants on the playground." That had made the knickers more endurable, but now that Big Buck was gone, the old embarrassment returned.

Wiping his tears, he walked toward the other buckeye tree shading the other front corner of their home. Kicking his foot through the ivy beneath it, he muttered, "Don't worry, Big Buck, I'll find us some double buckeyes; they haven't started dropping yet."

It was early September in the little town which hugged the hillside overlooking the steel mill and river beyond it. Although the days were still warm, the nights had turned cool, and football season was in the air. Steel Valley High's first game was only a week away. It was all the town talked about; it was all the men discussed while trudging up and down the hill, lugging their lunch pails, when crossing Oak and Main Avenues to the great gray mill that operated three shifts a day, seven days a week, fifty-two weeks a year, in and out of a bleary blanket of smog hanging halfway up the hill until nearly noon each day. The boy could never quite understand why the best homes—his home—had been built at the bottom of the hill when it was only the hilltop that remained above the smog. And he couldn't understand why everyone was more concerned about the coming football season than the war that already had taken several of their neighbors.

Yet, he was not completely immune to the town's football fever. He knew all the players—their nicknames, how much they weighed, how tall they were, what positions they played, and their strengths and weaknesses. He picked them out as they passed his house on their way to school each day. Rumor had it that the junior high coach was going to select a few seventh graders to practice with the team. Perhaps he would be one of them. Not that he was that good, even though people said he could run like a deer. If he were chosen, it would be because of his older cousin, Rip, who had been one of the best athletes ever to come out of the valley. The men often wondered aloud if he was going to be as good as his cousin. He didn't like that. If they wanted to compare him to anyone, it should be to Big Buck, his grandfather, who had played sandlot baseball in the old Southside league, and once had gotten a hit off Grover Alexander in an exhibition game. He wasn't even sure he had the courage to play football, to smash his head into a bigger boy, or to get crushed beneath a pile of players. It didn't matter, anyway, because baseball was going to be his game.

Nothing mattered much anymore, not since his grandfather had died nearly a month ago. The only thing the boy cared about, right then, was the promise he had made to his grandfather as he lay in the bed they had moved into the living room for him after his stroke. "This fall, I'll find us both a set of double buckeyes. Don't you be worrying none about that."

Double buckeyes—twin buckeyes in a single hull— were good luck charms more powerful than a rabbit's foot and lasting much longer than a four-leaf clover. He could still hear his grandfather, speaking weakly, but with a reassuring smile on his blue lips: "Never forget, double buckeyes mean double luck."

The boy remembered how his grandfather had helped him with his science paper; how they had gone to the town's new lending library on a cold January Sunday afternoon—the same lending library where his mother volunteered two nights a month; and how he had nearly burst with pride as he had later handed his grandfather the science paper with a big red "A" scrawled above his name. No one in the class, not even his teacher, Miss Baker, had known the difference between the scrubby little Ohio buckeye tree with its egg-shaped pod of puny buckeyes, and the true horse-chestnut tree. Except for him. And Big Buck, of course. Big Buck knew everything.

Genus: Aesculus, family: Hippocastanaceae, broad and dome-shaped, with long-stalked leaflets, and showy reddish-white bell-shaped flowers blossoming each spring—the best shade tree in all of North America. That was why Big Buck had planted them. He was no dummy. By fall each year, the flowers turned into clusters of prickly hulls each housing a single shiny buckeye. But every once in awhile, if you were lucky, you might find two buckeyes in a single hull. Double buckeyes! No one else in town had a horse-chestnut tree, and they had two of them!

The trees had been planted by the boy's grandfather at the turn of the century when their home had been built, and on the very same week when he had carried the boy's grandmother across the threshold of their new home. It was the first house in Steel Valley to be wired for electricity, even though the lines had not yet been run into the valley. But Big Buck knew they were coming.

When he had helped lay out the town in lots, people were surprised that a barber knew so much about surveying, compass readings, magnetic bearings, and sighting a transit. But if the boy had been there, he would not have been surprised. He could have told them that Big Buck could do just about anything.

"Another few weeks they'll be dropping, Big Buck. Then we'll have our luck back," the boy spoke aloud as he walked around the side of the imposing house, the biggest on their block.

Entering through the cellar door, the boy overheard his grandmother's concerned voice, "Absolutely not, Mercy. It's something he never needs to know!"

"But I worry, Mother, sooner or later he's going to find out. Wouldn't it be better if he heard it from us?"

"Never! I want your promise, right here and now, you'll never tell him."

"Well, if you think it's best," the boy's mother replied.

Pausing on the cellar steps, the boy wondered what they were talking about. Could it have something to do with him? Or his father? Or Big Buck? Or the polio that was frightening all the mothers in the neighborhood? Little Nathan Baily, who lived just six doors away, had come down with it, and Clarence Perkins, who lived in the next block, was rumored to have it, too. When the boy's mother had found out that he had been playing stick-ball with Clarence, she practically had become hysterical, burning the shirt and pants he had worn that day, and instructing him to cross the street rather than walk past either boy's home. No, it couldn't have anything to do with polio. He always kept his distance.

Perhaps his father had done something wrong, again. He was always getting in trouble with the boy's grandmother. After he had been called back to work, he had spent seventeen dollars of his first paycheck on a pearl necklace for the boy's mother.

"How could you do such a thing," Nan had snapped, "when we still owe money on our grocery bill!" That was probably it. His father probably had done something dumb again.

Entering the immaculate living room, graced by polished furniture and hand-painted vases, all precisely in their places, he looked at his mother and grandmother, shrugging, "No buckeyes yet."

"Did you wipe off your shoes?" his grandmother inquired.

"I always do."

"Oh, let him be, Mother. Come here, Little Buck, give me a hug."

"Aw, I'm getting too big for that, Mom," he hesitated until she walked over to him, squeezing him tightly.

"Go wash your hands," his grandmother ordered. "It's nearly six o'clock, dinner time."

"Yes, ma'am."

Seated in their Persian rugged, candle lit and lace-curtained dining room, eating from the delicately flowered china his grandmother had painted, atop the intricately patterned lace tablecloth she had crocheted, the boy picked at his food.

"Eat your dinner, Little Buck, and take your feet off the rungs of that maple chair," his grandmother admonished him.

"Yes, ma'am," he replied, unable to shake the empty queasiness that engulfed him ever since his grandfather's death.

As they usually did, his mother washed the dishes and he dried. Before his grandfather's stroke, the boy's grandparents had taken walks together nearly every evening after dinner. Sometimes they invited him to go along, and he would walk between them, strolling south along Oak Avenue—their tree-lined avenue—past the newer, brick homes owned by the town's most prosperous citizens. The boy had sensed a certain incongruity with a barber owning a home that was larger than the homes of the mill superintendent, the banker, the doctor, or the congressman. Their house was even bigger than the undertaker's, and he could show off three bodies at a time!

When Big Buck had died, Nan had said, "Putting your grandfather in the funeral parlor is absolutely out of the question. He belongs right here at home with us. And the money doesn't have anything to do with it!"

The boy was certain that she was right about keeping Big Buck at home with them, but he wasn't so sure the money didn't matter. Anyway, there was plenty of room, and the location of their home couldn't have been better. It sat in the center of the town's best block, on a little knoll overlooking the lesser houses.

Except for the plumbing and wiring, their home had been built by Big Buck and his brothers long before the others on the block, when land and lumber were inexpensive. It was just one more example of Big Buck's foresight. No one would have guessed that two barbers and a mouldmaker could have built it from scratch. Once when the lumber dealer delivered some boards for the new back porch, he just shook his head as he told the boy's grandmother, "That Buck of yours could have been a master carpenter, Victoria, I swear he could!"

Their stately home, along with its buckeye trees, gave the boy a special status on the block. There was no other like it. Spanning two lots, the two and one-half story white square house with its four white columns bracing a red roof over its long wide porch stood at the center of the block, holding the entire avenue together. The stained glass transoms above their windows were further proof of their standing. Even their address had a majestic quality about it: 111 Oak Avenue. Triple aces! An ace could count for one in blackjack, which he and Big Buck sometimes played for matches when they were alone. But pinochle really was their game. His grandfather had taught him how to play when he was six, and when his aunts and uncles came on Saturday nights, he always played his grandfather's hand for at least one game. Big Buck had taught him how to riffle the cards so the aces stayed on the bottom. But they only did that for fun. Yet, it was a good reason for always cutting the deck when someone else was dealing.

They always set up the card table in the living room, next to the marble-faced fireplace which was sealed shut at his grandmother's insistence.

"We're not putting up with dust from a fireplace now that we have steam heat," she had said. "Any woman who lets dust accumulate can't be much of a homemaker."

And dust was the ultimate enemy in their home. She went through their ten big rooms searching for it with a damp cloth and feather duster clasped tightly in her hands. She had her own little stepladder so she could reach the corners of their ten-foot ceilings, and she made the boy crawl around the furniture on his knees, wiping and polishing it, while his mother polished the table, china closet, and buffet.

The thirty-year-old Persian rugs in their living and dining rooms were vacuumed and beat until the boy expected them to fall apart. But somehow, they retained the richness of their maroon fabric, justifying his grandmother's claim that "They'll last a lifetime," which was another way of saying that even the rugs they walked on were better than their neighbor's.

Deep inside, the boy was enormously proud of their home, especially when he envisioned Big Buck climbing across the rafters, fitting the pieces of their red slate roof in place, and laying their hardwood floors, upstairs and down. The boy sensed that their home was much more than just a place to live. It was the center of their universe, a fortress that secured them from a cruel and dangerous world. And it really was all they had. In some ways, it owned them, he thought, consuming their energies, demanding their continuous attention, and absorbing their meager income. They seemed to exist, mainly, to take care of their house. Especially his grandmother, who wrapped her life around their home. Yet, it was a labor of love. It was their unique possession, one of the most important proofs that they were just as good as the more prosperous people in their town.

The other houses along their block only accentuated the special character of their home, like supporting actors clustered around the star. None were even half the size of 111 Oak, or at least it seemed that way. And inside, the dark, cramped clutter of their neighbors' rooms made 111 Oak sparkle. Not that they were run down and dirty, like the mill workers' match boxes on the hill, but things were seldom in their places, with unwashed dishes in the sink, or piles of sewing on the table, or clothes tossed carelessly across a chair. At 111 Oak, that absolutely never would occur!

The boy worried that their home badly needed painting, especially since the mill was once again belching out its fumes. The rotten egg-smelling sulfur from the coke ovens ate away at the paint, causing it to flake and peel, creating tiny crevices to which the soot from the blast furnaces would cling and smudge. But he shrugged it off when he realized that theirs was the only white house on the block. The drab grays and tans and inslebricks couldn't be compared. Anyway, his grandmother had said, "Wouldn't do for us to put money into paint during times like these. Why, what would the neighbors think?"

There was no doubt in the boy's mind that she would have had the house painted tomorrow if she could have come up with the money. And he was sure that the neighbors knew that, too.

Behind their home, in the distance, flowed the Monongahela River, and on the far bank, rising out of the water, stood a sheer cliff. On top of it, looming over the valley, there sat another steel mill, one dedicated to converting Steel Valley's ingots into sheet metal for tanks and trucks and ships and planes. Sometimes, when they went on their evening walks all the way to the baseball field at the end of the street, half a mile away, they could hear the clanging of steel, like the sour notes of a giant, broken bell, rolling across the level field, reverberating through their valley.

Nearly everyone called their baseball field the "dust bowl" because it was nothing more than a few barren acres of caked dirt between the mill and hillside. By the Fourth of July it was always as dry and dusty as the slag dump.

But Big Buck said that it was wrong to make fun of the field; it was what you did on it that counted. During football season, the dilapidated bleachers were shifted around and the pitcher's mound was leveled. That was where his cousin, Rip, had made his name.

Other evenings, they might stop to visit neighbors, or walk north to the old schoolhouse at the other end of town. They often talked of how they had strolled along the riverbank during the early years, sometimes even holding picnics there. In the winter, the river had frozen solid, and they had skated all the way across to the other side where they had built great bonfires on the bottom ledges of the cliff. Usually, at this point in their conversation Big Buck would wink and say that wasn't all they did, which brought a playful "shush" from Nan as she squeezed his arm. Around him, she was like a different woman.

Big Buck said that Nan had been the most graceful skater in the valley, able to make perfect figure eights going backwards, gliding like a swan. He also said that she had been the most beautiful girl in the valley, tall and slender, with rich long auburn hair. But that was no surprise. Big Buck wouldn't have married anyone but the best.

The coming of the steel mill ended their picnics and skating on the river. Its discharges, along with the growing town's raw sewage, filled the river and fouled the air. Sometimes, when the wind was blowing east, a stench from the river mingled with the smoke from the mill, hovering over their avenue, drowning their world in a pungent, dirty gray. But the boy didn't mind. He thought he was the luckiest lad on the face of the earth, until his grandfather died.

Since Big Buck's death, the boy's grandmother had gone into the living room after dinner each evening to lie on the couch with her left arm extended straight up in the air. This was an odd habit he couldn't understand, but she said it helped her circulation. She always claimed to be feeling poorly, especially since Big Buck's death. But she never looked sickly, and it never seemed to slow her down. She constantly complained of maladies ranging from near-diabetes to colitis, poor circulation to sharp pains in her head. Yet, she looked striking for a woman in her sixties. Tall and slender, with an imperious bearing, she was always well-dressed, and when sitting in her living room rocker she was ready to receive company by noon each day, even though they seldom came. Her snow-white hair was immaculately coifed and pulled back above her forehead to display her widow's peak.

"You know, of course, our widow's peak is a mark of beauty," she often explained to the boy when they were alone. "My father, your great grandfather, had one, but of us four girls, I was the only one to get it. And now, you. Always comb your hair back so it shows. You know, it was Tyrone Power's widow's peak that turned him into a leading man, and made him stand out above all those other actors. You're going to be a handsome man, too, Little Buck. Although I think you're probably going to look more like an Alan Ladd. Just always be sure your widow's peak is showing."

When visitors did come to call—she welcomed friends and neighbors like a queen receiving her subjects—she always insisted that Little Buck sit in the living room, listening to their conversation. "It's uplifting," she said. "You've got 'personality plus', Little Buck, and people have got to see it." The boy didn't know what she was talking about, but best he humor her, he thought. Eventually, she would get around to their widow's peaks, and how they were the only ones in the family with them. The more congenial guests usually replied, "Why, Mrs. Hart, now that you mention it, there is a striking resemblance between you and Little Buck. There surely is!"

Their observation would please her immensely, even though Little Buck would become flustered and embarrassed by her fawning over him in front of strangers.

Thank goodness we don't have any visitors tonight, he thought, as he put the last plate in the cupboard.

After lying on the living room Persian rug, thumbing through his baseball cards while his mother and grandmother knitted nearby, he finally excused himself, claiming he was going to his room to do his homework and then to bed.

As he kissed them both goodnight, his grandmother commented, "Well, I'm glad to see you're thinking about your school work for a change!"

Climbing the stairs, he heard his mother say, "Now Mother, you know he's getting good grades. Remember what Dad said, we don't want to make a bookworm out of him."

"Well, I just wish he'd study sometimes. That boy's in for a rude awakening. School's not always going to be that easy for him."

Once in his room, Little Buck looked out the window at the two buckeye trees bracketing their home. His thoughts returned to the promise he had made his grandfather, and to the days that lay ahead. Soon the buckeyes would be falling. He would be the king of the block, deciding who among his friends could be the first to hunt for buckeyes with him, determining what his share would be from each of their bags, standing guard over their ivy-covered front lawn as his grandmother chased away the high school students who tramped through the ivy searching for buckeyes. Even though he didn't know most of their names, except for the football players, he could tell a lot about them. He could easily spot the mean ones, carelessly trampling the ivy, pushing the others aside, ignoring his grandmother. And he could tell the good ones, too— the ones who were considerate, who smiled and apologized; some who even talked to him, tousled his hair and teased him about his freckles, asked *his* permission if they could take some buckeyes. But no one knew about the *double* buckeyes and what they meant. That was his secret, his and Big Buck's. He didn't even tell his closest chums, although one of them, Billy May, had seen his double buckeyes and asked about them. Perhaps he'd tell Billy May, he'd have to think about it some more.

Staring at his school books for a long moment, he tossed them in a corner, pulled his bulging stack of baseball cards out of his pocket, and threw himself onto his bed. Sorting through them quickly until he found Lou Gerhig and Elbie Fletcher, his two heroes. Gerhig, the Yankees' left-handed first baseman, who had a .340 lifetime batting average over fifteen seasons, and played 2,130 consecutive games before his terrible death. The "Iron Man" of baseball dying at thirty-seven. How could that be? And Elbie Fletcher, the left-handed first baseman of the Pirates, his and Big Buck's team.

The boy studied the two faces on the fronts of the well-worn cards, then turned them over, re-reading the statistics on the backs, closing his eyes and reciting them. Fletcher would never be a Gerhig, but he had led the league in walks, 105 of them. And Little Buck actually had seen Elbie Fletcher play—three times, six full games—on Sunday doubleheaders with Big Buck. He recalled the jostling trolley rides together, all the way to Pittsburgh, and the score cards which he penciled in with Big Buck's help, and the hot dogs, plastered with yellow mustard and smothered in white onion flakes. Big Buck had always let him eat as many as he wanted, along with bags of hot roasted peanuts and soda pop.

"Just don't tell your grandmother how many hot dogs we had, or we'll be getting a lecture about overeating," Big Buck had laughed.

The boy couldn't understand why Fletcher and Gerhig were not Big Buck's favorites. They were both left-handed first basemen like Big Buck had been, and like Little Buck was becoming. The entire family always made a big thing about Little Buck and Big Buck both being left-handed. And, of course, it was a big thing. Big Buck smiled every time someone mentioned it.

"We lefties are special, kiddo. Don't you ever let anyone tell you different," Big Buck had assured him. "Nobody can play first base like us. And we've got the edge on hitting, too."

"But they sometimes make fun of the way I write at school," Little Buck had complained.

"Don't pay any attention to them. They're just jealous, that's all. You're the only lefty on the block, aren't you?"

"Guess so."

"See. Just think how special that is. You're the only natural first baseman they have. And none of them can hit right-handed pitching like you. So who cares about how your writing looks, just so long as you get the grades."

"I suppose so," the boy shrugged.

Then Big Buck delivered the clincher. "Fetch the Bible," he ordered.

Reaching up on his tiptoes, Little Buck took the Bible from the mantle and handed it to his grandfather.

"Now, you open it to Judges 20:16."

Squeezing his eyes shut, the boy mumbled through the first six books of the Old Testament until he got to Judges. Then he thumbed through the book until he came to the proper chapter and verse. "Got it," he grinned.

"Read it out loud."

"*Among all this people there were seven hundred chosen men left-handed; every one could sling stones at an hair breath, and not miss.*"

"So you see, even back then, lefties were superior to all the men in the land," his grandfather nodded reassuringly.

"Whew! I never knew it was in the Bible!"

"So you can stop worrying about being left-handed, kiddo. Why, that just makes us special...a God given talent."

Although Little Buck was completely persuaded by his grandfather's explanation—after all, who could argue with the Bible—he still couldn't understand why Big Buck preferred Honus Wagner over Lou Gerhig. Gerhig was just as good as Wagner, and he was left-handed. Perhaps it was because Big Buck had seen Wagner play several times, and had actually met him at the Southside German Club. Everyone knew how Wagner bragged about being German. They even called him "The Flying Dutchman." But Gerhig was German, too. That should have made no difference.

Big Buck often talked about how his parents had come from Berlin, Germany. Although he had never been there himself, he could make it come alive, describing how his parents took Sunday afternoon strolls along the Unter den Linden, the widest street in the world, so wide that it had a park running through the center of it with manicured bushes and hedges laid out in circles, hexagons, triangles and squares. Women in their long, hooped dresses carried parasols just for show, and men in derbies and handlebar mustaches walked stiff-backed with gold-tipped canes.

Little Buck wasn't sure he understood why anyone would leave that kind of life to live among the steel mills, but he knew it had something to do with someone named Bismarck making all the young men join the army. Anyway, being German meant keeping your room neat—a place for everything and everything in its place—as Nan kept reminding him, and washing behind your ears, and letting your uncles give your head a "Dutch Rub" even though it hurt, and eating Limburger cheese with your grandfather on Saturday nights despite its awful smell, and sauerkraut on New Year's Day, and Dutch Cake on Sundays, and saying *Gesund heit*, when someone sneezed, and *Danke shoen*, when they said that to you.

Big Buck had grown up in that section of Pittsburgh where it was an accepted fact of life among the Germans that they were harder working, cleaner, neater, more disciplined, and generally better citizens than the other nationalities around them. And Little Buck had no reason to doubt his grandfather, for he was living proof of what he said.

"Be proud of your German ancestry, on both sides of your family," Big Buck had always told him. And he was, especially since it was the only thing about his father that his grandmother liked.

"Joseph Hart Helwig is a name you can wear with pride," she drummed into him, lowering her voice when she said his last name. Little Buck never doubted it, for he had been named after Big Buck—Joseph Hart. Although the name originally had been Hürt, with an accent mark above the *u*, Big Buck had anglicized it when he had moved to Steel Valley.

Their disagreement over Wagner and Gerhig was the only one they ever had. Although he had trouble understanding why he should be proud of being German when the country was at war against Germany, he could accept his grandfather's explanation: "We're fighting Hitler and the Nazis, not the German people."

He had helped organize the Junior Commandos on his block, part of a national organization of young boys dedicated to helping in the war effort. He and his buddies organized paper drives, going from door to door collecting old newspapers. They bundled and packed them in the old chicken coop behind his house from floor to ceiling. Two weeks after the truck picked up their first load, both he and Billy May were promoted to captain, and given a batch of Sergeant arm bands to pass out to their helpers. He was doing his part to fight Hitler, so he shouldn't be ashamed of being German.

But Wagner over Gerhig? Never!

Turning off the light and pulling his covers up around him, he lay still, watching the flicker of a streetlight from behind a buckeye tree. His thoughts returned to the conversation he had overheard as he was coming up the cellar stairs. Who were they talking about? What could it have been that they wouldn't want me to know?

Suddenly, the bizarre fantasy that had been playing around the fringes of his consciousness, ever since his grandfather's death, took on new meaning. Suddenly, he found himself confronting an idea that had been so absurd, so unthinkable, that he had driven it from his mind each time it had reappeared. Like a steel wire coiled tight around his skull, it gripped him until he thought his throbbing head would burst.

Could it possibly be true? His grandfather...his grandfather was still alive!

Chapter Two

Fantasizing

He had started fantasizing a few days after his grandfather's funeral. He had discovered that it eased the pain, the terrible emptiness, the numbing desolation that engulfed him. At first, he only pretended that his grandfather had temporarily gone away. Riding to the baseball field on his bicycle or sitting on the back steps alone, daydreaming, he would concoct elaborate scenes: Helping his grandfather pack for a trip to visit his brother in New York state, tagging along behind him to the train station, waving good-bye after his grandfather had slipped him a quarter, waiting for the mailman who delivered the postcards which came every few days from his grandfather.

"Having a good time. Uncle Bob and Aunt Nell send their regards. Tell Little Buck I miss him."

"Leaving tomorrow. Looking forward to seeing you all soon. Tell Little Buck to meet me Friday at six o'clock at the train station."

In his mind, he would be there early, pacing on the platform like a little old man, checking every few minutes with the ticket agent to be sure the train was still on time. When it finally pulled into the station, Big Buck's frame would fill the car's steps, ready to be the first one off.

Waving enthusiastically, he looked like he could have been the president of the United States stopping off at Steel Valley to say a word or two. He looked exactly as he had before his stroke: enormously dignified, yet bubbling with energy, his eyes dancing as though they held an amusing story that he would share only with you. When he grinned, people said he was the spitting image of General Eisenhower, except with hair. Little Buck had cut a picture of Eisenhower out of the newspaper, and had to admit there was a resemblance, even though it bothered him. Eisenhower didn't look anything like Alan Ladd.

In Little Buck's imagination, the day of his grandfather's return had been overcast until the moment Big Buck appeared on the platform. Then, the sun suddenly burst through, shining down from above the steel mill on the cliff across the river. When he closed his eyes and faced it, he could almost feel its warmth.

Despite the breeze, every strand of Big Buck's wavy, white hair was perfectly in place. Obviously, Uncle Bob had just trimmed it. Big Buck was wearing a pastel necktie that Little Buck had never seen, undoubtedly a gift from Uncle Bob and Aunt Nell. Although he could not see his grandfather's shoes, he knew they had to be shining. They always were. People said that he looked more like the president of the bank than the barber who cut hair in the basement underneath it. Alighting before the train stopped, Big Buck would lumber toward the boy, hug him and toss him high in the air, tell him how much he missed him, and then ask, "Got any new jokes for me?"

Big Buck was always prompting him to tell one of his jokes to the customers in the shop, or the men in the neighborhood, or at family gatherings, although Little Buck really didn't need any prodding once he had discovered that his jokes could capture people's attention and make them laugh. Grown-ups seemed to get a special kick out of a little boy rattling off jokes.

They were always egging him on. But his grandfather was his biggest fan.

He decided he would tell Big Buck the one about the fellow who shot his wife. When the fellow's friend visits him in jail and asks, "How long you in for?" He answers, "Two weeks." "Only two weeks for shooting your wife?" the friend shakes his head. "That's all," the fellow says. "Then they hang me."

Big Buck would throw his head back and roar. Together, they would walk from the train station, Little Buck insisting upon lugging the suitcase along the riverbank, then to Main Avenue where the bank dominated that most important corner of their town.

Big Buck passed the bank without even bending down to look through the basement window at his closed shop. "Tomorrow's time enough for that. Expect a mighty busy day. Bet they'll keep you stepping, too," he said, throwing his arm around Little Buck.

"Got my shine rags all washed and ready."

"Good. Best we're out the door by seven."

Turning right off Main Avenue, and then left onto their avenue—Oak Avenue—Little Buck called out to the neighbors sitting on their porches, "Look who's home. Big Buck's come back from his vacation."

All the neighbors would wave and greet him, some of the men even running down their steps to slap him on the back, to say how much they had missed him, how things hadn't been the same since he had gone away.

"I missed all of you, too, but Little Buck, here, most of all," he replied, nodding his head to accentuate his words, a trait that was his trademark. Although he had a tremendous air of dignity about him, a certain friendly confidence, he seldom held his head still when he talked. Perhaps it was because he couldn't use his hands for emphasis like other people when he was cutting hair. For whatever reason, he had a hundred different motions and expressions. If he lowered his head and furrowed his left eyebrow, you knew he was listening carefully and weighing your words. You had better know what you were talking about. If he smiled broadly, opened both eyes wide, and simultaneously gave his head a quick little nod, you knew he not only agreed with what you were saying, but thought you were mighty smart for saying it. But when he stood stiff as a dry razor strap, pursing his lips, staring at you blankly, his head tilted slightly back, you knew you were saying something awfully dumb. It took no words for him to tell you. Sometimes he even looked at customers or neighbors or folks at church that way. They, too, instinctively understood that they weren't quite making sense, but they never seemed to hold it against him. Instead, they usually asked for his advice.

"Well, what do you think, Big Buck?" "How would you tackle it?" "What do you say, Buck?"

But in Little Buck's fantasy, nobody had any questions to ask him on the day he came back from his vacation; they just were happy to see him, almost as happy as Little Buck.

When they reached their home, Little Buck ran ahead to let everyone know Big Buck was coming, and after he had hugged them all, he spread their presents on the table. He saved Little Buck's for last. A brand new, two-bladed knife perfectly balanced for mumbly peg.

They just sat around that evening, Big Buck smoking his Meerschaum pipe, occasionally refilling it from his Prince Albert tobacco can while he talked to the boy's mother and grandmother. Little Buck sat near him, on the Persian rug, listening to every word. The exquisitely curved pipe had come from Germany, and the creamy yellow bowl, with tiny carved fingers curling 'round the cup, was slowly deepening into a blend of amber red and dark cherry from years of hot tobacco tars seeping into the outer surface of the bowl and stem. Once the boy had asked his grandfather if he could have a puff, and although his mother and grandmother had objected, Big Buck just smiled and said, "Here, take a puff." Little Buck planted his feet firmly apart, wrapped his lips around the stem, and swallowed in some smoke. Suddenly, the room began to spin around his head and his stomach wretched. He felt as though he were going to die. His mother dashed into the kitchen to get him a glass of water and two saltines, which in a few minutes calmed his stomach and stopped the spinning room.

"Best you be careful what you're asking for, kiddo, 'cause sometimes you just might get it," Big Buck said, nodding his head knowingly.

As the weeks passed following his grandfather's funeral, Little Buck thought more and more about his grandfather being away on a vacation. At first, he told himself that it was only pretending, a way to pass the time and ease the pain. But occasionally, he caught himself actually believing the story, wondering when his grandfather would be coming home.

One day when he and his friend, Billy May, were riding their bikes to the baseball field, Billy said, "I guess you're still pretty broken up about your grandfather dying. I'm awful sorry, Little Buck."

"There's nothing to be sorry about," Little Buck snapped back.

"Well, I just thought..."

"Well, just stop thinking! Everything's going to work out fine. Nobody needs to feel sorry for me." He almost told Billy that his grandfather wasn't dead, that he was away on a vacation. But he was glad he hadn't when he realized how foolish he would have sounded. Billy had been to the house to see his grandfather. They had walked up to the casket together.

He was just beginning to accept the reality of his grandfather's death when he overheard the conversation between his mother and grandmother. Could that possibly be the secret? Could Big Buck really be away? Could his funeral have been a grotesque charade to cover up the fact that he was leaving them?

But why would he be leaving them? He had no reason. He loved them all. Even his father. His father and Big Buck got along just fine. On weekends, they worked in the yard together, or sat on the porch smoking their pipes, talking. Course, his father only had a straight stem store-bought pipe from off a card at Kramer's newsstand. They always went to Masonic Lodge together when his father was home. The boy knew he'd have to become a Mason someday because all the men in the family belonged. He thought it sort of strange that grown men took fancy little aprons with them when they went to lodge, and talked about "travelling in the east," and shook hands with each other in a funny way. But he figured it all had to have a good purpose if Big Buck did it, and he'd learn about it soon enough.

Sometimes his grandmother was awfully bossy, but that never bothered Big Buck. When she got on her high-horse, he just winked at Little Buck, threw his arm around her, and squeezed her tight. Only Big Buck could pacify her.

Every morning, they held hands as she walked him to the corner, carrying his blue lunch box that she had packed. They always parted with a kiss, a long one on the lips, right out on the sidewalk where everyone could see. Yuck! And she always was waiting at the door, watching for him, brushing her hair and putting on her lipstick, ready to hurry down the steps to take his empty lunch box and kiss him again.

Big Buck was extremely proud of her, the way she looked, and the way she kept house. "Don't let her bossing get you down," he always said. "Remember, everything she does is for us."

And he was always bragging about her artistic ability. Little Buck decided that his grandfather talked more about her painting than she talked about how Little Buck should behave. The shaving mugs in the big rack on the side wall of the barber shop all had been hand painted by her. Each one had the customer's name ornately lettered in the center, surrounded by curlicues and flowers. People said that the mugs were worth a lot of money. And her vases, china plates, and oil paintings were cherished gifts by everyone, perhaps even more so because she refused to sell them. That, Little Buck could never understand.

Once, a man who bought and sold art came all the way from Pittsburgh to see her paintings. He offered to buy the one she had hanging above the dining room buffet—the one of iris flowers with their petals blossoming in different shades of blue around tiny flecks of golden hair, all nestled among thin long leaves pointing toward the sky and setting sun, partly hidden by a thin grey cloud. He said that he'd take her other paintings on consignment, but she turned him down flat. She said it wouldn't be dignified, and what would people think if we were so hard up that she had to sell the paintings off our walls.

On one of their trolley rides to Pittsburgh, Big Buck had said, "You know, kiddo, we're mighty lucky to have our women. They don't come any better than your mother and grandmother."

"I suppose so," Little Buck had replied. "I just wish Nan wouldn't fuss over me so much."

"You've got to understand your grandmother, kiddo. Her whole life's wrapped up in us and our home. Sometimes she's a little tough on you because she cares so much. She sees herself in you. You've got her quick mind and restless energy. The reason you two sometimes butt heads is because you're so much alike."

"No we're not! I take after you!"

"Well, just don't be shortchanging your grandmother, kiddo. Never forget, for you, she wants more."

"What do you mean, more?"

"She wants you to make something of yourself. And there's no reason why you shouldn't. You've got what it takes. She doesn't want you ending up in the mill. Neither do I. We want you to look beyond the valley, get an education, and maybe become a doctor, or a lawyer, maybe even a congressman someday, like Augustus Felton."

"I'm going to be a barber when I grow up."

"No, you're not. I'd be disappointed if that's all you made of yourself."

"But...but it was good enough for you."

"That's the whole point, kiddo. What's good enough for me shouldn't be good enough for you. And what's good enough for you shouldn't be good enough for your children or grandchildren. Why, I expect you to be going off to college someday. I expect the name of Joseph Hart Helwig to mean something someday. We're all counting on you. Me, most of all."

Each time Little Buck thought about having his grandfather's name, he felt good inside, and he resolved always to use his full name, Joseph Hart Helwig. He wished he had told that to his grandfather before he had gone away.

No, Little Buck reassured himself, his grandfather couldn't have left because he was unhappy with the family. He cared too much about them all.

Perhaps he had left because he was in some kind of terrible trouble. But that made no sense, either. He was highly respected by everyone. He was chairman of the Board of Trustees at church. He could have been an elder, but he turned that down.

"Wouldn't feel comfortable wearing my religion on my sleeve," he had explained. "Taking care of the finances, making sure things run smoothly, that's more my style."

Men were always hanging around the barber shop, asking for his advice. On Saturdays, when Little Buck shined shoes, he liked to listen to their conversations.

Sitting on the straight-backed wooden chairs lining the shop, waiting their turns, the men would banter back and forth about the weather, or the Pirates, or Steel Valley's high school teams, depending on the season. They never talked about the war, except to mention when a local boy was transferred overseas, and then they lowered their voices as though he already had been killed or wounded. And they seldom talked about the mill, except to ask, "What trick you working next week?" Or, "You putting in for the second helper's job on number seven?"

Little Buck couldn't understand why they talked about everything except the two most important things in their lives: the war and their jobs.

When a serviceman came home on leave, Big Buck always gave him a free haircut, even though there usually wasn't much to cut. If it were a Saturday, Little Buck also offered him a free shoeshine. It was the least he could do for the boys defending the country, although he worried that they might all come home at once after the war ended.

Once, a Marine corporal showed him how to do a spit shine by applying a second coat of polish after the first was dry, sprinkling water on the tips, and then making the shine rag dance until his arms ached. The Marine explained that no shine could be considered perfect unless you put a dab of lanolin on the toes before the final few cracks of the cloth. Big Buck promised to order a tube of lanolin, and Little Buck added the spit shine to his repertoire for a nickel extra.

On Saturday mornings, Little Buck always could count on the undertaker and the congressman coming in for a spit shine, even if they didn't need a haircut. It surprised him, though, that he never could sell one to the banker. He even considered giving the banker a free introductory offer, but decided that it wouldn't be fair to his other customers, and they might find out. He tried varying his approach: "How about a first-class spit shine today, Mr. Clay?" Or, "Mighty fine looking suit, Mr. Clay. Spit shine sure would set it off."

But nothing worked. The banker would just grumble, "Clean 'em up, boy."

After inspecting each shoe carefully, turning it on its side and twisting around to see the heel, the banker would drop three shiny nickels into Little Buck's hand, one at a time, shaking his finger at the boy, "Waste not, want not."

Little Buck was proud of his shoeshines and disappointed when he couldn't persuade a customer to go for his extra touch. But try as he might, he never could equal the shine he saw on Frankie Rossi's shoes. Come to think of it, could Big Buck's run-in with Frankie be the cause of his disappearance?

Frankie was the town's chief numbers' writer. He wasn't just a runner though, like shriveled old Sabrina who flitted through the valley carrying her paper shopping bag, covering the businesses along Main Avenue and the nearby homes running along the bottom of the hill, or like one-armed Yunnick, who handled the hill. They worked for Frankie, and delivered their books and money to him each afternoon.

Supposedly, Frankie had other runners working for him, too, but Little Buck didn't know about that. All he knew was that Frankie Rossi was the best dressed man in town, his shoes always shined like glass, and his white Cadillac sparkled. He had considered asking Frankie where he got his shoes shined, but had decided it was a dumb question. Obviously, Frankie polished them himself. There was no place else in town to get a shine.

Little Buck often thought about Frankie Rossi, and especially about the Saturday morning when Frankie had asked Big Buck to become his partner. He was waiting for Big Buck, perched on the iron rail above the steps leading down into the shop.

"That rail isn't going to do anything for your cream pants, Frankie," Big Buck nodded, smiling.

"That's what handkerchiefs are for," Frankie smirked, sliding off the rail, pocketing the big white handkerchief that was underneath him, and tossing away his toothpick.

"You're not here for another haircut, are you?"

"Naw. Got an important proposition for you, Buck. Figured maybe we could talk before you got busy."

"Sure. Come on in."

"See you got Little Buck, here, for your helper."

"Yep. Couldn't get along without him on Saturdays."

"I'd like to speak to you in private, Buck."

"Well, come on back here in the alcove. Little Buck, after you set up your stand, fill up the lather jar and strap the blue razor."

As Little Buck went about his work, he could hear Frankie's hushed voice. "Got a great opportunity for the both of us, Buck. I've got a chance to pick up more of the valley, including the mill across the river, but I'll need a partner to handle my runners over here. Someone I can trust. I was thinking, with you located right here in the center of town, your shop would be an ideal place. Wouldn't take you but a few minutes in the morning to make the payoffs to the runners, and a few minutes in the afternoon to collect their books. Course, we don't write on Saturdays, so that would be a plus for you."

Dropping his voice lower, Frankie continued, "I'd bet you can clear more on the side with me than you take out of this shop after six days of hard work. You could even run your own book, right here in the shop. That would turn a pretty penny, too. What do you say?"

Big Buck gave Frankie his answer straight out, without any hesitation. "No thanks, Frankie. That's not my style."

"Suit yourself, Buck. You're passing up a chance to make some easy money." Swaggering out of the alcove, Frankie hitched up his pants, stuck another toothpick in his mouth, looked over at Little Buck, and said, "Say, kid, when are you going to learn how to shine shoes?"

"I already know how to shine shoes."

"Buy yourself a can of Esquire polish; it might help," Frankie snickered, flipping a quarter to Little Buck as he walked out the door.

"Keep your money," Little Buck shouted, throwing the quarter at the closed door as Frankie climbed the steps to the street, fortunately out of earshot for he was known to have a violent temper.

Standing in the alcove, his head tilted slightly back, staring blankly at his grandson, Big Buck asked, "Does it make you feel good, losing your temper?"

Little Buck shrugged and shook his head, embarrassed by his outburst. As he picked up the quarter and put it in his pocket, he mumbled, "You didn't take any guff from Andy Carnegie."

"That was different, kiddo. And what I did, I did courteously."

As a teenager, Big Buck had worked as a waiter at the prestigious Duquesne Club in Pittsburgh. One day, after having spent two hours waiting on Carnegie and several of his cronies in a private dining room, Big Buck received only a ten cent tip from the great steel baron, who loudly proclaimed, "Excellent service, young man. See to it that you're assigned to my table the next time I'm here."

Slowly opening the palm of his hand, Big Buck stared incredulously at the tiny dime as Carnegie strode out of the room. By the time Carnegie was walking down the steps of the club to his carriage, Big Buck had caught up with him.

"Excuse me, Mr. Carnegie, but you must need this worse than I do," he said, politely handing the dime back to the great man. Before the shocked Carnegie could respond, Big Buck turned and ran back up the steps into the club.

Little Buck loved to tell the story to his chums, to the boys in his Sunday school class, or to anyone who would listen. And he felt within his rights for not letting Frankie Rossi make fun of him.

"How come you didn't take Frankie up on his offer?" he asked his grandfather.

"You want me to be a numbers' writer? Would that make you proud?"

"Course not. Just wondered why you passed up a chance to make some easy money."

"Easy money's hard money, kiddo. Don't you ever forget it."

"But you play the numbers sometimes."

"Playing them's one thing. Booking them's something else."

"If playing them's okay, how come Nan made such a fuss last Christmas Eve when she found out Pop was playing them? Especially since he won?"

"Oh, don't pay her too much mind, boy. You know she means well."

Little Buck would never forget the explosion that had occurred in their home on the previous Christmas Eve. Uncle Bob and Aunt Nell had just arrived from New York state with their two sons and daughters-in-law, and Rip and his wife were there along with Rip's sister, Emily. The colored Christmas tree lights cast a soft glow through hundreds of glittering icicles, each one having been hung meticulously on the ten-foot blue spruce by Little Buck and his grandfather. The living room was filled with happy chatter and the mixed aromas of pine scent, mincemeat pie, and turkey stuffing when a knock was heard at the front door.

It was old Sabrina, the numbers' writer, in her sagging black stockings and sneakers, clutching her dirty paper shopping bag, her toothless smile dominating her shriveled face.

"Allan here?" she squeaked, surveying the happy family.

"He's right here, Sabrina. Come in and get out of the cold. And a Merry Christmas to you," Big Buck roared, as Nan frowned at him.

"Can't stay but a minute, Buck. Making my rounds, with some good news for Allan. You hit 314 today for a nickel, Allan," she said, shuffling across the room to Little Buck's father, and counting out $42.50 as she placed it in his hands.

Thanking her, he thrust four dollars back into her hand, as was the custom, and smiled sheepishly, "Guess today's my lucky day."

"And how many unlucky days have you had, Allan, that we don't know anything about?" Nan hissed, glaring at him.

Little Buck's father glared back at her, turned abruptly and left the room.

"I don't know what we're going to do with him, squandering his money like that," Nan said as she looked disgustedly at Little Buck's mother.

"All right, Victoria. That's enough," Big Buck calmly said. "Why don't you get us another pitcher of eggnog?"

Everyone was subdued for the balance of the evening, and after Little Buck was in bed, he heard his grandmother's voice in the hallway, "So that's where his money goes. No wonder we can't make ends meet."

Little Buck didn't like the way his grandmother always picked on his father, yet, he admitted to himself, what she said usually made sense. But she wouldn't think of criticizing Big Buck, even though he often put a nickel on the numbers. Anyway, the important thing was that Big Buck had turned down Frankie, cold. Easy money wasn't Big Buck's style.

Word spread that Big Buck had turned down Frankie. By the time Billy May's parents heard it, the story had Big Buck throwing Frankie out of the barber shop. Although Little Buck knew that was not what had happened, when Billy May told the story to his chums as they sat on the curb in front of Billy's home, Little Buck simply smiled knowingly. He was so proud that he thought he would burst.

When Frankie stopped getting his haircut at Big Buck's, and his Cadillac began appearing every afternoon across from the bank, in front of Mac's barber shop, that confirmed the rest of the story: Mac had taken on the local numbers' racket as Frankie's chief lieutenant in the valley.

Little Buck wondered if Big Buck's refusal to get involved with the numbers had anything to do with his going away. But people get into trouble by going into the rackets, not by staying out of them, he reasoned.

The boy thought so hard his head ached, trying to imagine what terrible problem could have driven his grandfather away. He thought about it in school. He thought about it on the playground. He thought about it in bed at night. Suddenly, one morning just before dawn, about the time the starlings started chirping on the porch roof, he sat straight up in bed. He was certain he had his answer. Finally, he knew why his grandfather had to leave them. Big Buck had had no other choice.

Chapter Three

Facing Facts

The mortgage! That had to be it! They were behind again, and the bank was going to foreclose. But
the bank couldn't foreclose on Big Buck if they couldn't
find him. At the very minimum, his disappearance
would cause a long delay. Big Buck had outsmarted
the bank by going away. And he had done it for the
family.

About the time Little Buck and his parents had
moved in with his grandparents, his grandfather had
had to take out a mortgage on their home. His grandmother talked about it incessantly.

"It's hard to believe," she sighed, "that we've come
to this. On the day your grandfather carried me through
that door, this house was paid for. We didn't owe a
red cent to anyone! And now, having to borrow money,
just to live. You'd think men would have the decency
to stop getting their haircuts and shaves if they didn't
have the money to pay for them. Or at least would put
a little something down."

"This Depression can't last forever. They're good
people; they'll pay when they get the money," his
grandfather had assured her.

"Well, it's mighty hard to swallow, incurring all
these new expenses without any money coming in,"
she had said, looking at Little Buck's father.

The boy always felt so guilty. If only his father hadn't lost his job. But then, he wouldn't be living with Big Buck. That was worth almost anything. And Big Buck never complained about it. Never said a word. Instead, he always insisted that it was terribly wasteful having only two people living in a ten-room home.

"Why, when your mother got married and moved out, this big old house was like an empty barn," Big Buck had explained. "Truth is, when your mother moved away, it gave me a awful homesick feeling. Watching her grow up was my special joy. From the time she was a little girl, she was the sweetest, kindest little thing you could imagine. And she hasn't changed, not one bit! So, when you folks moved in, I got back your mother, and you, kiddo, which were my big bonus of two joys instead of one. And your dad, too. We get along just fine. Don't pay any attention to what your grandmother says about him. He's a good man. I just think he missed his calling. With the way he can sing and play the piano, he should have stuck to music. But, I guess your Grandpap Helwig wanted him to follow in his footsteps in the business. Lord knows, he shipped him off to the best of schools. But when the Crash wiped out your Grandpap Helwig—and killed him, too—I think it took something out of your father forever, even though he was a young man at the time. But I can tell you this, kiddo, he loves you and your mother something fierce. And we get on fine, too."

There was no doubt in Little Buck's mind that his father and grandfather were the best of friends. Together, they were vital to the neighborhood. Twice a year, in spring and fall, they pushed Big Buck's huge, homemade, cement roller over every lawn on the block. Everyone agreed that the lawns along Oak Avenue looked like velvet because of Big Buck's roller. But it posed one problem. It was too heavy. Big Buck had constructed it by filling a fifty-five gallon oil drum with concrete, inserting a steel pipe through the center of the concrete before it set, and attaching a U-shaped steel handle to the pipe. No two men on the block could move the massive cement cylinder more than a few feet at a time, and even that required the most terrible grunts and strains. Some couldn't budge it at all.

Together, laughing, Big Buck and his son-in-law would strip off their shirts and heave their perspiring bodies against the handle, pushing the roller down the cindered alley into the yards of all their neighbors. Each lawn was rolled from front to back, and then, side to side, with their neighbors running ahead of them, scattering grass seed, while the women stood on the porches, waiting with their gingersnaps or oatmeal cookies, and lemonade.

Little Buck's father wasn't quite as tall or heavy as Big Buck, but his muscles rippled, probably from all those years on the open hearth. Little Buck tagged along behind them on their grass-rolling days, basking in the reflected glory of their prodigious feat, yet also worrying that he may never have the strength to take his place beside them, to do his share. He also wondered if the neighbors had mortgages on their homes, or if they were in trouble with the bank. But he was always afraid to ask his chums for fear they would find out about the mortgage on 111 Oak.

Nan never came right out and blamed Little Buck and his parents for the mortgage, but he could see it in her eyes, in the way she looked at them when she talked about it.

Could they be behind again? Times had picked up since the war began. Big Buck's shop was humming again, and the boy's father was working, too. Yet, the mortgage was the only logical explanation. They couldn't take the home away from Big Buck if he wasn't there. That had to be it. Only Big Buck would have been smart enough to figure that out. And only Big Buck would have been willing to make such a sacrifice for his family.

But it wasn't right for his grandfather to be living alone, hiding somewhere in a rooming house without clean sheets or home-cooked meals or people to love him. He would find Big Buck! He would go to him!

There was so much Little Buck wanted to tell his grandfather; so much that had been left unsaid before he died, or went away. Their last moments together were seared into his soul. After the doctor had told the family that Big Buck's death was only hours away, they had permitted Little Buck to enter the converted living room for one last time. The two sets of wooden sliding doors, separating the hall from the living room and the living room from the dining room, were tightly shut, eerily accentuating the pale yellow glow from the single night light setting on the mantle above the bed. Although the sun was shining brightly outside, the heavy maroon drapes pulled across the windows made it seem like the dead of night. Their once happy living room had become a chamber of gloom, smelling of disinfectant, and shrouded in shadows.

He could hear his grandfather's heavy breathing and see his pallid face within a semicircle of pale light, which cast down across the pillows.

In the background, he could hear his mother, Nan, and Cousin Emily sobbing. In the adjacent hall, his father, Cousin Rip, and Uncle Bob, who had driven all night to get there, stood silently, wiping their eyes with their handkerchiefs. Little Buck decided that in the history of the whole world, probably no one had ever been loved by his family as much as Big Buck. And Little Buck was certain that he loved his grandfather more than did any of them.

When Big Buck opened his eyes and smiled at him, he swallowed hard and tried to smile back. He hoped Big Buck couldn't hear the women crying.

"Don't forget our double buckeyes, kiddo," his grandfather whispered, weakly. That was when Little Buck promised to find a pair that fall for each of them.

There was so much more that Little Buck wanted
to say. He wanted to tell his grandfather how much he
loved him. He wanted to throw his arms around Big
Buck, hug him, and hold him tight. But he was afraid to
say or do anything that might make Big Buck realize
just how sick he was. So he only laughed about how
all the men's hair was growing down over their col-
lars, waiting for Big Buck to get back to the shop. He
even considered telling Big Buck a joke, but decided
that wouldn't be appropriate. He found that he could
hold his tears back by clamping his jaws shut, and
wished that the women in the background had learned
that trick.

Big Buck just patted the boy's hand, and then
closed his eyes. They said he slept away sometime
that night.

After Big Buck died, or had gone away, it gnawed
at Little Buck that he had not been more serious during those last few moments with his grandfather, and
that he had not told Big Buck how he really felt.
Everytime he thought about it, it brought back a dull
ache that he feared might never go away.

He had to find Big Buck! He had to tell him how
much he loved him. Yet, how could he find him? Nan
would never tell. But, surely his mother also knew,
and she never could say "no" to Little Buck. He would
pry it out of her.

Washing dishes one evening, he whispered, "How
come Nan doesn't complain anymore about the mortgage? Is it paid off?"

"Heavens, no. It won't be paid off for another fifteen years. But at least we're not behind. Don't you be
worrying about such things, Little Buck."

"What do you mean, we're not behind? How could
we be making payments now that Big Buck's gone?"

"Oh, your father's been making them ever since
he went back to work. Thank goodness for that."

"I see," Little Buck mumbled, his lower lip quivering, disconsolate that his theory had been shattered.

In the weeks that followed, he tried to accept his grandfather's death. Each time he walked into their reconstituted living room, he saw his grandfather's coffin blocking the mantle, smelled the sickly, sweet odor of dead flowers, heard the whispered condolences of their friends and neighbors, and the teary-eyed sniffling of his great-aunts and cousins. He saw his mother, sitting on one of the funeral director's folding chairs, speaking softly, smiling wanly, trying to hold herself together. And his grandmother, practically collapsed in the big sofa chair, letting out short bursts of sobs each time she tried to speak. For the first time in his life he had felt sorry for her. Such a thought had never even entered his mind before. She was always so self-assured, so precise and proper, so much in control. Not only of other people, but of everything around her—the furniture was exactly the style and color scheme that she thought best; the curtains hung precisely as she said they should; the food was cooked as she required, never fried and never fatty; the lights were dimmed at dinnertime; they ate to the Victrola's soft strains of a Strauss waltz or a Mozart sonata; and smoking was absolutely never permitted at the table. Yet, she always set out Big Buck's pipe and Prince Albert can on his smoker next to his chair in the living room after dinner.

Little Buck remembered how she had looked, sitting near the coffin: confused, unable to fully comprehend what had happened. Yet, she was dressed as immaculately as ever. Her long pearl necklace matched the three-stranded bracelet on her wrist. Her black suede pumps—the ones he had cleaned so many times—blended with her black silk dress. Every hair was perfectly in place, and her widow's peak seemed to glisten in the dimly lit dead room.

Of course, Big Buck was dead, the boy told himself. Everyone saw his body lying there. Little Buck recalled the vigil—the night he had sat up near the casket with his great-uncle. His mother had objected, but his grandmother had insisted, "It will be good for him. It will help him remember his grandfather."

So he did it. Not because he needed anything to help him remember Big Buck. He was astonished that his grandmother would suggest such a thing. Obviously, she didn't understand. He did it because it meant he could be with Big Buck for eight more hours. That was reason enough. And he was proud that he hadn't fallen asleep, not even for a few minutes. Uncle Bob had dozed on and off all night. Initially, Little Buck sat on the couch next to Uncle Bob. Then, he sat on one of the undertaker's folding chairs so he could see his grandfather's face. Then, he moved to another chair so he could see his grandfather's hands and body. Then he walked to the casket so he could touch his grandfather for one last time. But he decided not to. He remembered how cold his grandfather's hand had felt when his grandmother had made him touch it. The bulging blue veins of his right hand—his glove hand—seemingly had grown larger. Strangely though, his swollen knuckles, battered by years of sandlot baseball, appeared to have shrunk, and his stoved and twisted fingers were as stiff as popsicle sticks.

No, there was no need to touch his hand again. He would never forget how it had felt.

That night, with his Uncle Bob, he was determined not to fall asleep. He remembered how he had fallen asleep in the same living room, on the same living room rug, during the first Louis-Schmeling fight. His grandfather had carried him to his room and tucked him in bed. The following morning he had been too ashamed to look at anyone. Big Buck had spoken up for him, reassuring his mother and grandmother that he was old enough to stay up late to listen to the fight. And he had failed his grandfather!

The next morning, when Big Buck told him that Schmeling had knocked out Louis in the twelfth round, he worried that it might have been his fault. He and Big Buck both were rooting for Joe Louis, even though Max Schmeling was a German.

"The Brown Bomber's an American, kiddo, so we better stick with him," his grandfather had said.

He hated himself for falling asleep. It was one of the most embarrassing experiences of his life. And his grandmother had made it worse by saying, "I told you he was too young to stay up so late. And just because he fell asleep on the floor doesn't mean he got his proper rest." He had stared down at his bowl of shredded wheat, said nothing, and was mortified.

Two years later, he had decided to make amends. He begged them to let him stay up to listen to the second Louis-Schmeling fight. As usual, his grandfather prevailed, and he was allowed to gather around the radio with the rest of the family.

Although he was rooting for Louis again, he was bitterly disappointed by what occurred. Louis knocked out Schmeling in two minutes and four seconds of the first round. No one would ever know if he could have stayed awake for the entire fifteen rounds.

Sometimes, nothing works out right, he thought. But then, he was proud that he hadn't fallen asleep during the all-night vigil at his grandfather's casket. He hoped Big Buck knew.

Thinking about that vigil, remembering the ghostly pallor of his grandfather's face, and the clammy feel of his cold hand ultimately forced Little Buck to confront the truth.

He got on his bike—a secondhand twenty-six incher with a rusty dent in the front fender and missing chain guard, which he had purchased for six dollars from Greeky Karris's older brother and promptly painted fire engine red—and pedaled ferociously up Oak Avenue to the cemetery at the north end of town. Dismounting, he wiped the sweat from his forehead with his sleeve and pushed his bike ahead in the direction of the Hart family plot. Reaching it, he rested his bike on the kickstand, and paused momentarily, lowering his head because that seemed like the thing to do at the graves of his great-grandparents and Uncle John, Big Buck's elder brother and the father of Rip and Emily. Then, he cautiously raised his eyes in the direction of Big Buck's grave, wincing, almost afraid to look.

Inching toward the fresh mound of clay-colored dirt, he felt a terrible weakness consume his entire body. He swallowed hard and then shook himself. That seemed to help a little. Steadying himself on the Hart family headstone, he studied each of the individual small gravestones set in the ground around it. They even had a gravestone for Big Buck's baby sister, who had died at birth. Then he stared at the clump of dirt supposedly representing Big Buck's grave. "Don't even have a gravestone on it," he muttered. "Don't prove nothing, except that they dug a hole." Tears welled up in his eyes as he stiffened his body and clamped his jaw shut tightly. Turning, he ran across the graves of his great-grandparents, jumped on his bike, and raced toward home with the wind stinging his wet cheeks.

A few days later, the bank rented the shop to a barber from Coalton, who didn't even move to town. Nan sold everything in the shop except the shaving mugs and the shoeshine box, which Little Buck kept. He begged his grandmother to keep one of the Kokin barber chairs, just in case Big Buck was still alive. But she shrugged, "What use would we ever have for a barber's chair?"

When she asked Little Buck to deliver some of their oldest shaving mugs to Big Buck's dearest customers, he knew all hope was lost. Big Buck never would have let them give away his shaving mugs. And what if his grandfather's customers handed them to the new barber? Or, even worse, to Mac? Little Buck could never let that happen!

Chapter Four

Discovering the Dream

Reluctantly, he took the shopping bag filled with shaving mugs, each carefully wrapped in newspaper upon which the customer's name was written in red crayon, and started on his journey on a brilliant September Saturday afternoon.

He decided to make his first deliveries to the homes of his closest friends—Tubbo Grimes, Tucker Ramsey, Shrimpy Cox and Billy May—reasoning that Big Buck's neighbors would be least likely to turn over their mugs to the new barber. After all, they still would need his roller for their lawns. He also wanted to practice his spiel first on those he knew best.

At each door, he announced that he had a very valuable gift from his grandmother, and then paused, waiting to be invited inside, hoping that his presentation inside their home would make the event seem more important than a mere delivery at the door, and would also increase the possibility of his seeing both husband and wife. Once in the living room, he carefully set his shopping bag on the carpet, tried to flash his best smile, and then ever so gently reached into the bag and withdrew the proper mug, carefully unwrapping the newspaper around it.

He tried to remember everything his Cousin Emily had told him about her selling techniques, for she had been the best salesman ever, while at Nathan's Shoe

Store in nearby Coalton before she got her chance to work for Gimbels in the city.

"I always hold only one shoe at a time in my hand," she had confided to him, "on the tips of my fingers, delicately, as if it were a priceless, beautiful object, uniquely suited for that particular customer. And I smile...always smile and nod your head 'yes.' It's amazing, Little Buck, but if you nod your head 'yes' to people, you can get them unconsciously nodding, too. Never underestimate the power of suggestion."

And, of course, Little Buck was trying to sell something. Not for money. But that just made the challenge more exciting. He was trying to sell an idea, trying to persuade his grandfather's oldest and dearest customers, without ever actually saying the words, that they should not turn over their shaving mugs to another barber.

"Nan said she knew that Big Buck would want you to have this mug as a keepsake," he spoke softly, even reverently, as he held the mug up on the tips of his fingers. "Course, we're only giving away a few of them, to Big Buck's closest friends. You might even want to plant a flower in it," he nodded affirmatively in the direction of the woman, his blue eyes dancing above his best broad grin.

"Why, of course, Little Buck. What a wonderful gesture...how thoughtful," each of the neighbors replied.

Satisfied that he was subtly getting his point across, Little Buck continued on his errand along Oak Avenue, cautiously stepping over May's disgorged and broken sidewalk, uprooted by a gnarled white oak, delivering the precious shaving mugs to the town's most important citizens. Everyone seemed genuinely touched, and assured him that they would treasure their hand-painted mug as a prized memento.

Even Mr. Clay expressed his deep appreciation, although Little Buck couldn't understand why his grandmother would want to give such a priceless object to the man who held their mortgage, who insisted that the shop rent be in his hands by the tenth of every month—even in the worst of times, when Big Buck couldn't make ends meet, and who refused Little Buck's earnest sales pitch for a spit shine. There was something wrong, something *too much* about one individual holding the strings to both your home and your business. Little Buck wasn't sure why he thought it was wrong, but he decided that he would never let himself get in that position. He would make enough money to protect himself and his family against hard times so he could never be destroyed by them, like his grandfather Helwig, or be embarrassed and worried like Big Buck.

Yet, money wasn't all that mattered. When Big Buck had talked of Little Buck making something of himself, he had never even mentioned money. That was odd, considering how strapped they always were. And Big Buck never pointed to Mr. Clay as an example, even though he was the richest man in town. It was always the professional men—the doctors, the lawyers, a certified public accountant who lived across the river, or the congressman—to whom Big Buck referred when he spoke of Little Buck's future.

From Big Buck's encouragement came the boy's dream of what he could become, stirrings deep within his consciousness, slowly taking shape. First, he would become a big league baseball player, a first basemen, and then, well, he wasn't sure. If Big Buck didn't want him to become a barber, perhaps he should become a lawyer. People always said he could talk the pants off anyone. He figured he got that from his Cousin Emily. He usually was chosen to play the most important role in their school plays, or give the class speeches at their assemblies. He liked being in the center of things, yet, it had its drawbacks, too. He worried that he might be tagged a "teacher's pet," although he felt that his boisterous conduct in the classroom and on the playground probably saved him from such a humiliating fate.

Nan claimed that he had "personality plus," although he decided that what she really meant was that he should work harder at developing it.

One thing he knew for certain was that he loved telling jokes. When he was about eight, he discovered that he could make grown-ups laugh at his stories. In the barber shop on Saturdays, or on the church lawn before Sunday school, or on the street corner men would cluster around him and urge him on. He sometimes thought that they got a bigger kick out of his telling it than from the joke itself. But that didn't bother him. And Big Buck always urged him on. Even Nan smiled a little at his jokes, as long as they were clean.

He thought about being a comedian, but decided he didn't look funny enough; and then he considered being a preacher, but decided he wasn't good enough. Whatever he would be, he would become a community leader like Big Buck, taking an interest in other people, helping them with their daily problems, talking with them, encouraging them. Little Buck often found himself thinking about his future, wondering what he would become, when he walked or rode his bicycle along the southern end of Oak Avenue, where the town's most prosperous people lived.

During the afternoon of his shaving mug deliveries, when he reached the combined home and office of Dr. Carver, their family doctor, he paused to look through the windows of the doctor's Cadillac, parked in the driveway. Each time he saw the sleek black sedan, with its showroom-clean interior, it nearly took his breath away. Equally impressive, was the "C" gasoline ration sticker on the windshield, which meant the doctor got all the gas he wanted!

Once admitted to the stately brick home, he noticed that the furnishings and decor were not nearly as impressive as at 111 Oak, and an odor of disinfectant, or perhaps formaldehyde, wafted from the direction of the doctor's office, where he heard the noise of wailing babies.

Although the doctor was too busy to see Little Buck, his wife thanked Little Buck and assured him she would write a note to the boy's grandmother that very evening.

As he resumed his errand, stopping to peer inside the doctor's Cadillac again, his nostrils still held the faint stench of formaldehyde, and he could hear the distant crying of the babies. Running his fingers along the polished surface of a fender, he muttered, "Don't believe I want to be a doctor, that's not my style."

Approaching Augustus Felton's stone home at the end of the street, he hesitated, wondering whether he should deliver the mug to the front door or to the congressman's side office. Noticing lights on in the office, he climbed the stone steps, read an "open" sign on the door, and entered.

He took a seat on a wooden chair against the inside wall of the crowded waiting room to wait his turn. He watched the people filing in and out, and through the thin wall could catch most of their conversations. An elderly Polish woman, dressed in widow's black with a babushka tied tightly over her head, pleaded in broken English for the congressman to get her only son released from the service because her husband had just died. The high school fullback, flanked by his parents, asked the congressman to help him get an appointment to the Naval Academy. A local service station owner needed an increase in his gasoline allotment. A peg-legged man felt he was being cheated out of his railroad disability. Finally, it was Little Buck's turn.

Even though he had shined Augustus Felton's shoes many times, and had carried on easy conversations with him about the Pirates, or the Steelers, or their hometown teams, he could feel his heart pounding wildly as he entered the congressman's spacious office. Behind a massive mahogany desk sat the great man himself, looking a hundred times more important than he had sitting with his pant legs turned up, atop Little Buck's shoeshine stand. On the wall directly behind him was the great seal of the United States, bracketed by two large flagpoles from which hung the American and Pennsylvania flags. A side wall was filled with photographs, including one of Augustus Felton sitting at a dinner table next to President Roosevelt, and another of him dressed in Army fatigues, talking with General Eisenhower and several other officers in a clearing overlooking wooded, rolling hills. Big Buck did, indeed, look a lot like General Eisenhower, with his hat on.

"Afternoon, Congressman," Little Buck grinned and tried to appear relaxed.

"Why, Little Buck Hart. I sure have missed you on Saturday mornings, boy. What brings you here?" Augustus Felton, smiled, walking around the desk to shake his hand. Little Buck firmly grasped the congressman's hand and squeezed it hard, the way Big Buck had said he should. The boy almost blurted out "Helwig," but caught himself. There was nothing to be gained by correcting the congressman, especially since most of the people in town called him "Little Buck Hart," and he sometimes wished it were his name.

As he went through his speech about the shaving mug, he realized he was much more nervous than he had been in the homes of Big Buck's other customers.

Smiling, the congressman held the mug up to the light, turned it slowly, and commented softly, "Why, that American flag waving in the wind looks as smooth as silk, and that Pennsylvania flag, why, she's got all the detail, even the gold fringe around the edge. Bet you don't know what those words below the flags mean."

"Sure I do," Little Buck stiffened to attention, "*E Pluribus Unum*...From Many, One."

"Good for you. I better be watching my step or you're going to be after my job. Now you be sure to tell your grandmother how much I appreciate this. Why, that Victoria, she should have been a professional painter. Don't forget to tell her I said that," the congressman waved his finger at the boy.

"Yes, sir."

He thanked Little Buck profusely, placed the shaving mug in a prominent position on a corner shelf, and walked Little Buck to the door. Just before Little Buck left, with his heart still pounding wildly, the congressman took his hand, patted it and said, "I was terribly sorry about your grandfather, Little Buck. I never knew a better man."

Little Buck nodded awkwardly, made his way through a delegation of what appeared to be coal miners standing in the waiting room, and leaped off the stone steps down onto the sidewalk, flying his empty shopping bag like an airplane, high above his head.

Although the sun was still hovering above the steel mill on the cliff across the river, the air had turned nippy, and the streets were deserted. It was nearly supper time, but Little Buck was in no hurry. He had to digest the experiences of that afternoon. So he cut through one of the yards to the alley behind Oak Avenue where he could find large cinders and hurl them at garbage cans on his way home. Pinging cinders off the sides of cans, he suddenly realized that his old energy had returned for the first time since his grandfather's death. Nearing his home, he flung a handful of cinders at a garage roof to scare the starlings off it, and then paused, leaning against the garage to watch the sun setting behind the distant steel mill. Just as it disappeared, leaving a reddish glow above the cliff top, overlooking the river and the valley, Little Buck raised his head and whispered to the sky, "Someday, I'm going to be a congressman!" and then turned and ran toward home.

Chapter Five

Sweet Sundays

Little Buck told his grandmother that everyone seemed to appreciate their shaving mugs, and he had the impression that they intended to save them as keepsakes, rather than give them to a new barber for use when they got their shaves.

"Just so Mac doesn't get his hands on them," she snapped.

Nan was even pleased that a new barber was coming to town because it meant that Mac would not automatically be getting Big Buck's customers. But Little Buck resented a new barber using Big Buck's shop. He swore he would never patronize him.

Little Buck never could understand why his grandmother hated Mac. His mother had explained that Mac had once worked for Big Buck, and had actually learned the trade from him. But that hardly seemed like a reason to hate the man.

"There was a time when Mac was like a big brother to me," she had said. "Your grandfather took him into the shop when he was about your age. He started out just like you—shining shoes, cleaning up, and lathering. Back then, shaves were even more important than haircuts. Some of the business and professional men got shaved every day. Eventually, your grandfather taught Mac the trade, showing him how to trim and layer, so a man could get windblown and his hair would fall right back in place."

"Then how come we don't like him?"

"Oh, it's not that all of us don't like him. Leastwise, I could never find it in my heart to dislike him. But after he got accepted into the Guild, he stayed with your grandfather for about a year, and then set up shop across the street. Didn't make any of us happy, but your grandmother...well, she actually despised him for doing it. She hasn't spoken to him for over twenty years."

"What did Big Buck think about it?"

"He'd never discuss it, except to say, 'It's a free country.' That really set off your grandmother, so you best not be mentioning it."

"Is that why Big Buck always got his hair cut in Pittsburgh when he went to Guild meetings, after Uncle Bob moved away?"

"I'm sure it is. Course, your grandmother trimmed it every Sunday morning, but we don't talk about that."

Sunday mornings, sweet Sundays. They seemed so empty now that Big Buck was gone. Little Buck remembered how his grandfather always came in to wake him; how they tiptoed downstairs before anyone else was up; and how his grandfather let him have his own cup of coffee soup. That was Big Buck's breakfast every day, and on Sundays Little Buck could join him. The mixture had to be just right: A steaming mug of coffee, three-quarters full, with a splash of cream from the top of a milk bottle before it was shaken up, two heaping teaspoons of sugar, and one well-toasted slice of whole wheat bread, that was broken into chunks and soaked in the coffee for about thirty seconds before you began to eat.

Then, Sunday Dutch Cake for everyone else who came down to breakfast. When he was younger, he somehow had the impression that his grandfather got the Dutch Cake from Germany each Saturday night.

But now he realized that it came from the local bakery. Several times when he had been in the bakery shop, he had studied their Dutch Cakes, but he never could find one covered with clumps of brown sugar as big as the ones his grandfather brought home, clumps as big as clay marbles, some even as big as purgy shooters.

If Little Buck's grandmother came downstairs and caught them, she never failed to admonish both of them. "Don't you two know that coffee's bad for you. It'll eat out your insides. I'm surprised at you, Joseph. You'll stunt the boy's growth."

But Big Buck always placated her. "Come on, Victoria, just a half a cup won't hurt the boy. It's Sunday."

Little Buck never understood why his grandfather could get away with dunking Dutch Cake, but when he did it, his grandmother practically had a fit. "Stop that, Little Buck! You're never going to learn how to eat out in polite company if you practice table manners like that here at home."

Big Buck would wink at him and say, "She doesn't know what she's missing, does she kiddo?" as he dunked another piece up to his second knuckles.

Sweet Sunday mornings: Everyone dressing in their best clothes, primping, and bustling through the house to get to church on time.

Little Buck thought he would burst with pride, walking beside his grandfather on their way to church. His mother and father usually walked in front, and his grandmother usually staying home, insisting that she alone would cook their Sunday dinner. Because it was the most important meal of the week, she probably felt only she could prepare it to perfection. And she probably was right. Little Buck never understood how she could be so domineering with everyone else, yet insist upon waiting on Big Buck practically like his slave.

"Can't stand that new Presbyterian preacher, anyway," she had said, excusing away her Sunday absences.

"He can't be five feet tall, and he prances back and forth beside the pulpit in his pinstriped pants and tails like the headwaiter at a Rockefeller wedding. Why your grandfather ever let them choose him, I'll never know."

Little Buck thought the preacher shouted a lot, but aside from that, he seemed all right. Anyway, he remembered his grandmother saying, "It's the congregation that makes the church, not the minister. It's our church, not his. Preachers come and go, but we're here to stay." So he couldn't understand why she let him bother her so much.

Church was the highlight of Little Buck's week, even more than catching baseball in the alley with Big Buck, or sitting on the porch, listening, as Big Buck explained to everyone why it was important to invade Europe through Italy, or why Roosevelt should run for a third term, even though Big Buck hadn't supported him before. Church was where Little Buck confirmed his family's special status. Church was where *everyone* saw just how important his family really was.

It started in Sunday school, in the John Hart Memorial Class, named after Big Buck's dead brother, who had taught the class for nearly thirty years. Rip, his son, who was Little Buck's older second cousin, was the teacher now. People were amazed that Rip had turned out so well. Caring about nothing in high school but sports and girls, he had just squeaked through, even though he was supposed to be bright. In the yearbook, his quote under his picture was, "Basketball is what you play when there's too much snow on the ground to play football." He was a halfback, and had led Steel Valley to two consecutive undefeated seasons. In one game against Coalton, he had scored five touchdowns, an unbroken school record. People said he should have gone to college, but instead, he went to work in the steel mill, and played semi-professional football for the Olympics. People said that he was drunk on the night he ran off with one of his girlfriends and got married. But they also said that after he came back, he was an entirely different person. He stopped drinking and got a job on the county police force. He even stopped swearing. Little Buck tried to remember if he had ever heard Rip curse, but the worst he could come up with was "cripes." Rip said that a lot, but nothing more.

Eventually, he was promoted to detective, and when his father died, took over his Sunday school class. All the boys admired Rip. Parents never had any trouble persuading their sons to go to Sunday school. He spent more time talking about sports than about the lesson, unless you counted such subjects as good sportsmanship, and fair play, and trying hard. His favorite saying was, "If you can't say something good about someone, whistle." When you tried to talk to him about the Pittsburgh Pirates, especially to defend Elbie Fletcher's fielding, he whistled a lot.

Sitting in a circle with his Sunday school class, in the basement of their church, listening to Rip explain the lesson, Little Buck often thought, "He may be the teacher for us all, but only I'm his cousin!"

Rip and his wife, who had no children, were always inviting Little Buck to their furnished apartment above the clothing store. They always produced a box of Stouffer's creme chocolates from which he had his pick. Then, Rip would bring out his scrapbook and they would spend the afternoon reliving Rip's exploits: The clippings of each Steel Valley game in which he played, the box scores from the Industrial League when he caught for the mill, and the team pictures of the Olympics and the stories of his feats. Rip could describe particular plays that had occurred years before: How he had spun away from three tacklers on a right end sweep, or held on to the tag at home despite a spike gash that required eleven stitches. Then he always showed you the scar on his left arm. Little Buck loved to leaf through the scrapbook, to get Rip to explain the importance of each game. Yet, there seemed to be something sad about having your glory days behind you when most of your life was still ahead. He decided that an important difference between Rip and his sister, Emily, was that Rip was always talking about the past and she was always talking about the future. But Rip was still his hero, next to Big Buck, of course.

Little Buck decided that if his grandfather had ever had a son, he probably would have looked a lot like Rip, his nephew. Rip had Big Buck's round face and wavy black hair. Little Buck hoped that he would look like Rip when he grew up, but his hair was blond like his father's, and his face was oval-shaped like his mother's. That worried him.

Exactly five minutes before the close of Sunday school, Little Buck was permitted to slip upstairs, all the way to the belfry, to help his grandfather ring the church bell. Big Buck would boost him up so he could grab hold of the bullrope and dangle from it as, together, they clanged the bell. He never understood exactly why they rang the bell when the church service was about to begin. If anyone heard it in his home, he would not be able to get to church on time, unless he lived only a few doors away. But he loved to hang suspended from the bullrope, above his grandfather, as the bell peeled, resounding through the belfry until his eardrums vibrated and his arms tingled.

Little Buck knew every room, every corner, every cranny of their church. Sometimes he liked to climb the side stairs to the primary room and sit on the little children's chairs where he had learned to color and recite his first Bible verses. Being too big for the miniature chairs and tables made him feel grown-up and important.

He knew where the cloths for dusting the pews were kept; where the Christmas ornaments were stored; and where the paper for the bulletins and the ink for the mimeograph were kept. He could find his way in the dark to the switch box in the church kitchen, where he helped his grandmother during the fall and spring church dinners. Somehow, it didn't seem right that she should be in charge of such important dinners when she seldom went to church. But the Ladies Missionary Society always insisted. The Rotary Club said they would move their Monday evening dinners to the Presbyterian Church if Victoria Hart would run them, but she declined, saying Monday was Big Buck's day off, and, anyway, she couldn't afford the time away from home. She said that people didn't appreciate how much planning went into preparing a full course dinner for a hundred people. She would be busy for weeks before the fall and spring dinners, discussing the menu with the ladies of the church, negotiating with the grocers, counting the pots and pans and plates and utensils, and scrubbing everything including the undersides of the folding chairs and tables. That was Little Buck's job. On the evening of the dinner, he usually helped set the tables and scrape the plates afterwards. Whether his grandmother had served turkey with all the trimmings, including warm plum pudding sauce, or sliced ham with a pineapple ring and cherry in the center, everyone raved about her cooking. Once the preacher said she could open up a fancy restaurant in Pittsburgh. When she told him, "Why, I believe you'd just like to get rid of me, Reverend." He shot right back, "Can't get rid of what I hardly ever see, Victoria."

After ringing the church bell on Sunday mornings, sometimes, if it looked like it was going to be a busy day, Big Buck would let Little Buck help him pass out bulletins. But he always slipped into the pew next to his mother before the service began, sitting on the end next to the right aisle so he could clearly see his grandfather as he took up the collection on that aisle. Big Buck always winked when he handed Little Buck the collection plate. Even though Little Buck knew the wink was coming, he always grinned sheepishly, simultaneously hoping that no one had noticed Big Buck's wink, yet also hoping that everyone had seen it. When the ushers carried their collection plates up the two aisles and stood in front of the pulpit, they all looked a little drab and faded compared to Big Buck, who practically sparkled from his newly trimmed hair and starched white collar to the tips of his Nunn-Bush shoes. Not even the undertaker, who worked the other aisle, was as spiffy as Big Buck.

But Little Buck's grandfather didn't just pass the plate. He was responsible for the whole collection. Little Buck knew every step of the procedure: How Big Buck counted the money after church with the preacher and undertaker looking on; how he made out the bank deposit slip and they initialed it; and how he put the money and slip in a canvas pouch and held it up while the preacher snapped the lock shut. The bank had the only key. Big Buck had insisted upon it, saying, "It's not my style to handle other people's money unless they can see that it's secure." He thought of everything.

Only Little Buck knew where Big Buck hid the money which was under his mattress until he could deposit it on the following day. Little Buck always worried about letting any of his chums come upstairs with him on Sunday afternoons. If they had a good reason, like trading baseball cards or swapping shooters, Little Buck always pulled the door closed to his grandparents' bedroom. You couldn't be too careful with all that money in the house.

Midway through the church service, after the collection, the choir always rose to sing the anthem. By the time they got around to the anthem, Little Buck was so proud of what already had occurred, that he could hardly sit still in his seat. And then when the choir stood up, if his father wasn't working, he nearly always was the star. In the black robe his mother had ironed the night before, his father stepped forward to the center of the loft, above and behind the preacher, to sing his solo, or at least a duet with the preacher's wife. His father's soft blond hair seemed to shimmer as rays of sunlight filtering down through the stained-glass windows danced upon it. His clear tenor voice filled the church, reaching the high ceiling, floating up into the back balcony and through the open windows to the street beyond. His father seemed to come alive when he sang or played the piano. People said he had missed his calling.

Before the war, he had been the tenor soloist in a glee club, singing at church socials and community events up and down the valley. His grandmother said it was a terrible waste of time. No stag party was complete without his father playing the piano and singing ribald ditties. One of the neighbors had told Little Buck, "Your father's not the life of the party...he's the whole party." Little Buck wasn't sure he liked that.

Although Allan Helwig couldn't read a note of music, he could play the piano by ear. If he didn't know the tune, all someone had to do was hum it. He'd stumble through it once, and by the second time, you would have thought he had composed it.

One Sunday, when the organist took sick, his father spent the Sunday school hour picking at the organ, humming through the hymns. By church time, he was up there on the organ bench above the choir, playing the prelude like the master organist at a great cathedral.

When Little Buck's grandmother heard of his father's organ playing feat, she simply muttered, "What a fraud." She said that his singing and piano playing were just another way to avoid responsibility. Little Buck wondered if she didn't stay away from church because of his father's prominence. From what he could surmise, it appeared that his grandmother had never forgiven his father for not making a lot of money.

"Your father had every opportunity, and he squandered it! Don't you ever do that," she had pounded into his head. "Private schools...the best of everything...and ending up in the mill. What kind of a man is that?"

Apparently, Little Buck's Grandfather Helwig had built up several thriving businesses, but had been destroyed by the Great Depression. Leaving the farm as a teenager to clerk in a general store, he eventually had opened a store of his own along the river, about twenty miles south of Steel Valley. He expanded into real estate and insurance, and opened one of the first nickelodeons in the valley. People said that he built it so his little boy, Allan, could sing during the intermission, as was the custom of the day. He never denied it, nor the stories that he was responsible for the bouquets of red roses showered upon his son at the conclusion of each performance.

Victoria Hart thought they were getting the catch of the valley when Allan Helwig, Jr. started calling on her daughter. People still talked about the wedding she had thrown. Everyone knew it had been her idea to hold it at high noon in the living room of their home, rather than in church. She had claimed it was the fashionable thing to do. Little Buck had seen the pictures of it with flowers everywhere: on the mantle, across the window sills, up the banister of the stairs, in the bridesmaids' hands, and in Cousin Emily's hair. She had been the flower girl. The ushers, in their striped pants and long-tailed coats, wore strange wide ties and white gloves. Rip, especially, appeared ill at ease, one foot twisted awkwardly atop the other. But Little Buck's mother and father looked like they belonged on the cover of *LIFE* magazine. She was radiant. Petite, yet well-proportioned, she looked like the pretty cheerleader she once had been, her big dark eyes sparkling beneath her black bangs. Obviously, Big Buck had bobbed her hair that morning. The long train of her wedding gown was spread around in front of her.

Little Buck wondered how she had been able to walk down their circular staircase without tripping.

He had never seen his father looking so serious, or so well-scrubbed. His usually soft blond hair was plastered down, probably from a dose of Vitalis, and his most distinguishing feature, the rippling muscles of his body, was completely hidden beneath the layers of his formal wedding clothes. That must have pleased Nan, Little Buck thought. His grandmother always complained that his father looked more like a riverboat roughneck than a member of one of the valley's most distinguished families.

Apparently Nan had never gotten over Grandfather Helwig losing all his money. Almost as if she had a right to some of it for accepting his son into her family. And then, when Little Buck's father went to work in the mill, it was more than she could bear.

Little Buck tried to understand why she hated his father so, but he never fully could. And when his father stood up in church on Sunday to sing the anthem, all he could think of was how proud he was of his father's musical ability, of his grandmother's artistic ability, of his Cousin Rip's athletic ability, of his Cousin Emily's sales ability, of his mother's extraordinary kindness, which was her special ability, and most of all, of Big Buck, his grandfather, whose abilities were unlimited. Little Buck worried that he had none of their abilities. He had tried to paint a picture once of a stream running through an autumn forest, but his grandmother had to show him how to make the sunlight fall upon the turning leaves and dab the shadows on the ground beside them. It was a mess. He couldn't carry a tune, and the few piano lessons he had taken were a disaster. He had none of his family's natural talents. Well, maybe only baseball, but now that Big Buck was gone, there would be no one to bring him along, to cultivate what little ability he just might have.

During the Sunday sermons, when his grandfather was still alive, Little Buck's thoughts usually turned to his family and how lucky he was to have them all. He always loved the sermon, not because he listened, but because he could daydream without fear of getting caught. As the preacher excoriated the congregation to cleanse themselves of sin, he would see himself playing first base for the Pirates, with Big Buck cheering in the stands, or cutting the ribbon at the opening of his six chair barber shop in Pittsburgh's William Penn Hotel, with Big Buck proudly looking on.

But now, none of that could ever be. Big Buck was dead. To the boy, it was a calamity far worse than the Great Depression or the war. Those two disasters had struck everyone, and seemed so distant by comparison. But Big Buck's death had struck him, alone. There was no one to share his misery with, not his mother, not his father, or his grandmother. They couldn't understand. No one could understand how he felt, so it made no sense to try to tell them.

Little Buck took a deep breath and sat straight up. The important thing, he told himself, was that he had had his grandfather for the first eleven years of his life. He was Big Buck's only grandson. Not another man on earth could ever make that claim!

Chapter Six

A Valuable Lesson

The day he dreaded most was fast approaching. Although his grandmother had trimmed his hair, she had already mentioned that he needed a full cut, and that it would be good to patronize the new barber. The thought of walking down the steps to his grandfather's shop made him sick at the stomach. Maybe he could go to Mac's instead. He had always wanted to get to know Mac. He was fascinated by the stories his mother had told him of their childhood together, how Mac had done the very same jobs that he had performed for his grandfather, back in the early days when Big Buck was a young man. He wanted to hear those stories firsthand, to know what it was like to be around Big Buck when he was starting out.

Big Buck had often described the early days: How the men had piled into the shop for shaves on Saturday nights; how he sometimes stayed open until two o'clock on Sunday mornings; and then how he carried his loaded pistol in his belt as he walked home alone, along deserted streets, with a paper bag filled with money stuffed inside his shirt. The gun still was in his grandfather's dresser. Little Buck wondered if Mac knew about the gun, if Mac had stayed until the shop closed, and if his forearms had ached on Sunday mornings. Even if Mac couldn't tell him anything new, it would be good to hear the same old stories again, almost as if Big Buck were there to tell them.

But Nan would never let him go to Mac's. She couldn't even hear his name without exploding. On the second evening when Big Buck had been laid out, around dinner time before people were supposed to come, Mac had appeared at the side door. Nobody but the family ever used that door. Guests called at the front door, and Little Buck's chums, as well as tradesmen, came to the back door. When Little Buck had answered the knock on the side door and had discovered Mac standing there, suddenly, he had realized how close to the family Mac once had been.

"Evening, Little Buck. Awful sorry about Big Buck. Wonder if I could speak to your mother?"

Little Buck's mother heard his voice and came down the stairs. "Evening, Mac. How have you been?"

"Oh, pretty fair, Mercy. How about you? Awful sorry about Big Buck."

"Good as can be expected, I guess."

"I was wondering if, maybe, I could pay my respects before the crowd starts coming. That is, if it's okay with Mrs. Hart. I wouldn't want to rile her up at a time like this, and I know how she feels about me."

"Wait here while I speak to her."

When Nan heard that Mac was at the side door, her grief-stricken sobbing abruptly stopped. Bolting out of her chair and down the stairs, she thrust her finger in Mac's face so suddenly, Little Buck feared she was going to poke his eye out.

"Don't you ever set foot in this house!" she hissed at him.

"Get out, get out, get out," she waved her arm hysterically, backing him out of the doorway.

"Mother, Mac's only here to..."

"We don't need you here for anything. You're not welcome in this house, you...you traitor. Get off our property! Now!"

Holding his hands up in front of him, Mac backed away, turned, and grumbled over his shoulder as he left, "I only came to pay my respects. Someday you'll get yours, Victoria Hart."

"I'm so sorry, Mac...," Little Buck's mother called after him.

Recalling the frightening incident, Little Buck decided it would be futile to ask if he could get his hair cut at Mac's. It would probably just set off his grandmother again.

Finally, on a Saturday morning, his mother laid two quarters on the table in front of him. "You're looking awfully straggly, son. Why, Big Buck would be ashamed if he saw that hair of yours. Best you get it cut for church."

He couldn't argue after the way she put it. So he nodded, scooped up the quarters, and went out the side door. Pausing in front, he studied both buckeye trees. "Cripes, they're late this year, he muttered."

From the porch across the street, Billy May called him, "Hey, Little Buck. Hear the good news? Come on over here."

Several of Little Buck's chums were talking excitedly, crowding around Tubbo Grimes, slapping him on the back.

"What good news?" Little Buck asked dejectedly, walking across the street, stuffing his hands in his pockets.

"Tubbo's getting called out Monday. The coach told his older brother, after practice yesterday."

"Says there are two other seventh graders on the list," Tucker Ramsey added.

"Did your brother say who they are?" Little Buck asked, trying to appear nonchalant.

"Naw, but everybody figures you're one of them. List is supposed to be on the bulletin board Monday morning."

"Don't make any difference to me," Little Buck shrugged, kicking at a loose brick. "Not even sure I want to play."

"Don't give us that baloney," Shrimpy Cox sneered. "You'd kiss the coach to be called out. Course, if we had a Cousin Rip, we'd have nothing to worry about either."

"You're just mad 'cause your in the eighth grade and they still haven't given you a uniform, Shrimpy," Billy May spoke up.

"Yeah, Little Buck's faster than any of us, so I say he deserves the chance," Teddy Knox nodded.

All the boys, except Little Buck, ran off in the direction of the vacant lot, tossing a football among them, pushing and shoving each other. He stood watching them for a few moments, and then crossed to his side of the street. Walking slowly along the avenue, he mindlessly studied each home, each porch, each piece of pavement on the sidewalk. He knew them all by heart: How the screen door on Teddy Knox's front porch had to be jerked to be opened; the kitchen cupboard where Shrimpy Cox's mother hid her oatmeal cookies; the broken pavement in front of Sniveley's where you had to jump your bike across; and old man Schmidt's lawn that eventually everyone refused to cut because he cursed at you if you didn't pull all the crabgrass. Little Buck knew every inch of his block. He could have walked it blindfolded; he even knew the insides of most of the homes. And he knew all the families, each person old and young, and the stories that went with them: How the Mays and Schmidts had moved to Steel Valley around the turn of the century, about the same time as the Harts; how old man Schmidt and his wife had refused to take in his widowed sister; that Percy Kauffman had been a "love baby" according to Nan, although that was something you were never to talk about; and what time Dolly Cox took her bath each night, and where the older boys stood in the parking lot to watch her get undressed.

Little Buck liked hanging around with the older boys, with Nails and Shoes and Brain. Shoes, especially, was his friend. Shoes went to the Presbyterian Church, too, and although he was in the senior high Sunday school class, he always had time for Little Buck. Shoes was entering the eleventh grade and already had earned varsity letters in football and baseball. That was almost unheard of in Steel Valley. There was talk that he might be moved from end to halfback for the coming season. Little Buck and Big Buck had agreed that that would be a good decision. Shoes was the fastest boy in school. During baseball season, he practically owned center field. Little Buck wondered if he was going to be as fast as Shoes.

Some of the older boys didn't like Little Buck tagging along with them to the ball field, trying to get in on their pickup games in the vacant lot, or just sitting with them on the curb, listening to their conversation. But Shoes always made him feel welcome. "Little Buck can be on my side," he would say. Or, "Little Buck can be our lookout," if they were planning a victory garden raid.

Throughout the summer and into the fall, the boys of Oak Avenue raided the gardens that grew along the riverbank. Because the gardens were on vacant land, more than a block away from the nearest home, the raids were not particularly risky. Usually, the boys would wait until dark, and then enter, crawling on their hands and knees through the sweet corn, stuffing their paper bags with corn, tomatoes, carrots, potatoes, or whatever else might be in season. Then they would build a fire in the vacant lot between Petersons and Schmidts where they would roast their corn or potatoes in the hot coals, or toast their carrots on a stick.

Sometimes, on Friday nights, when the bakery rolled long racks of bread into its open garage to cool,

Shoes would suggest that they hook some hot bread. Although Nails and Brain usually claimed it was too risky, Little Buck never hesitated.

"I can do it! I can cross down by the railroad tracks, crawl in there, load up a bag and be out in ten seconds—between the time they bring one cart out and go in for another."

"Well, Little Buck is smaller than we are," Brain would say.

"Yeah, Little Buck, you go do it. We'll be your lookouts," Nails would urge him on.

His willingness to do just about anything they asked, cemented his relationship with the older boys and gave him a special status with his own chums.

Often he would lead Billy, Tubbo, Shrimpy, Teddy, and Petey on forays of their own into a garden at night, or occasionally to hide in the shadows of the parking lot, watching Dolly Cox get undressed to take her bath. They could only do that on nights when her brother, Shrimpy, wasn't with them.

For the boys of Oak Avenue, their various incursions represented more than idle mischief. Their daring deeds demonstrated, at least to themselves, that they were as tough as the boys from the hill, the sons of the immigrant steel workers. And Little Buck's reckless courage somehow helped make up for his having to wear knickers and use good English and keep his hair combed.

Lingering along the sidewalk, dawdling on his way toward the center of town, Little Buck caught a glimpse of Brain's garage behind his house.

* * * * * *

Once, when the older boys held a boxing match in that garage, with gloves and ropes held by four boys serving as corner posts and a referee and a real stopwatch, they asked the younger boys to join in. Everyone agreed, so an entire afternoon of boxing was arranged. Each boy was matched with another of about the same age and weight. Each bout was scheduled for three rounds, and no one got too badly scuffed until they got to the final fight of the day. Brain, as the promoter of the event, had decided that Tubbo Grimes should fight one of the older boys because of his enormous size. It only became clear toward the end of the afternoon that Brain was saving Tubbo for himself.

Brain Conlon was the meanest boy on the block. He acquired his nickname, certainly not from his sparse intelligence, but from the shape of his head and the absence of any hair thereon. Each spring, Brain's father had insisted that Big Buck shave Brain's head and, of course, Big Buck had done as he was asked. You didn't build up your trade by arguing with your customers. Once shaven, the contours of Brain's head exposed a slight hump running from the center of his head down to the base of his skull. Even if he had not been the meanest boy on the block, his bald head and oddly shaped skull created an aura of sullen anger. His empty, ice-blue eyes conveyed a bestiality, a certain wanton brutality, accurately portraying his inner feelings.

Brain wanted Tubbo Grimes. They were the only two left who hadn't fought. Brain had seen to that. It was his garage. And Tubbo had at least twenty pounds on Brain, even though Brain was four years older. There was no way Tubbo could get out of the match without being called a coward. His eyes darted frantically from Little Buck to Tucker Ramsey to Billy May and back again to Little Buck, with sweat pouring out of his pimply face as Nails fitted on the gloves, tying them securely.

Brain stood in the opposite corner, sneering fiendishly, pounding his gloves together, dancing up and down.

"You ready, Tubbo?" Nails asked, moving to the center of the ring.

With that, as Tubbo tried to nod, tears welled up in his eyes, his mouth dropped open, and he heaved out his spaghetti lunch upon the floor.

"What some sissies won't do to get out of a fight!" Brain excoriated the hapless boy, while his friends cleaned up the mess and led him to a wooden crate where he slumped, sniveling, in teary-eyed disgrace.

"All right, who's got the guts to put the gloves on with me now? Nobody, I suppose," Brain shuffled around the makeshift ring, jabbing the air. "You're all a bunch of sissies!"

"Cripes! I'll fight you," Little Buck shouted, grabbing the gloves and thrusting his hands in, one at a time.

"Now, hold up, Little Buck," Shoes said, jumping into the ring, "there's no need for that. We've all had our fun. I'd take him on myself if Nails and I hadn't already gone at it. You've had your fight. Let's just call it a day."

"I haven't had my match yet. Let him fight if he wants to, if he's not a puking sissy like that tub of lard there in the corner," Brain taunted.

"Let them fight," Nails insisted, and so the fight was on.

Climbing into the ring, Little Buck felt a surge of adrenalin pumping through his body, and he could almost hear Big Buck whispering in his ear, "Keep your guard up, feint and jab."

With the dull clang of the angle iron, Little Buck rushed across the ring, faked a right jab at Brain's jaw, and caught him in the ribs with a solid left hook. Grimacing, Brain danced away, resuming his fiendish grin. He let Little Buck pursue him to the far corner, flailing wildly at the bigger boy. Suddenly Brain froze, and then started slowly shuffling forward, relentlessly jabbing at Little Buck's face and body. At first, Little Buck tried to stand his ground, throwing his whole body into a flurry of wild swings, but Brain's fists drove past his guard like sledgehammers through slate, with a devastating two-step rhythm: wap-wap, left-right, wap-wap, thump-thump; wap-wap, left-right, wap-wap, thump-thump.

Reeling backward, trying to regain his balance, Little Buck refused to dance away, but each time he attempted to hold his ground, Brain pummeled him. He felt a terrible sting, and then a swelling in his left eye, a thud to his stomach that made him cough and gasp for breath, and a sharp jab to the center of his face and then the taste of warm blood gurgling through his teeth. He bounced against the ropes as a blow to the stomach doubled him over. His knees buckled as he flung his arms around Brain's elbows, tying him up at the sound of the angle iron.

Shoes and Billy helped him to his corner as Shrimpy shoved a crate beneath him. After sponging him off and wiping the blood from his face, Shoes turned around and said, "Okay, that's enough. You've had your fun, Brain. You win."

"What do you mean?" Little Buck shouted, jumping up. "You can't stop the fight. He didn't even knock me down!"

"Let the little punk fight; you're not his mother," Brain sneered, dancing to the center of the ring.

"Ring the bell," Little Buck ordered, spitting a hocker of blood through the ropes.

As the second round began, he cautiously circled, keeping his distance from the older boy. Each time Brain led with his one-two rhythm, Little Buck tried to counter with a single jab. Neither were connecting until halfway through the round, when Little Buck tried to follow up one of his jabs with a right to the kidneys. Brain took the blow and then responded with a round-house left, knocking Little Buck across the ring into the ropes. Bouncing off the ropes like a raging bullock, he lunged at Brain, flailing the air as his opponent easily slid away.

Once again, Brain suddenly stood firm, and pummeled Little Buck with his vicious one-two rhythm. Standing toe to toe with the older boy, Little Buck landed a solid blow for every four or five that he took, but he was still swinging wildly, his face bloodied and his ribs battered, when the round ended.

"I got him figured out," he gasped to Shoes and Billy as they sponged him down and smeared vaseline on his cut face.

"Come on, Little Buck, let's just call it a day. No need for you to go out there again. You've won just by staying on your feet."

"I'm telling you, I've got him figured out. If I stay away from him, and then move in and out quickly, that'll be my style. Counterpunching alone won't work," he wheezed, as the angle iron sounded for the final round.

Keeping his distance, they sparred back and forth for the two minutes of the round. Little Buck's sudden attacks and quick withdrawals could not penetrate Brain's defenses, nor could Brain get to Little Buck, who bobbed and weaved and danced away.

When Brain missed three punches in a row, Little Buck crouched down and charged, butting his head into Brain's chin and pummeling his midsection with his flying fists. Instead of reeling from the blows, Brain simply tucked his elbows in tight and covered his face with his clinched fists. Between his gloves, on Brain's lips, their appeared a distorted, demented smile, then his ice blue eyes seemed suddenly to come alive, nearly bursting out of their sockets, frenzied and deranged.

He struck a hammer blow right through Little Buck's gloves to his jaw, and then another to his ribs, and then like a relentless jackhammer, into his face and ribs and face again. Against the ropes, Little Buck did not fall to the concrete. Rather, he slowly sunk to it as Brain kept punching him. Even as one of his knees touched the floor, Brain delivered a final smashing blow to his skull. Little Buck's body sprawled limply at Brain's feet.

Little Buck saw a blur of sneakers dancing over him, and heard Nail's voice, counting, off in the distance, "One...two...three...."

That was all he could remember. When he woke, he was lying in a corner of the garage, covered with blankets, and a wet towel wrapped around his head. All the boys were hovering over him.

"You're a good little fighter, kid," Brain leered down him, punching him lightly on the arm.

"You okay, Little Buck?" Shoes asked.

As Little Buck opened his mouth to answer, he felt a sharp pain in his cheek and a swirling nauseating dizziness in his head, so he swallowed hard and nodded.

After they propped him up and gave him a tin cup full of water, he tried to speak. "Guess I didn't do too good, huh?" He could still taste blood in his mouth, and when he talked, the skin on his face smarted and his jawbone ached.

"What do you mean? Why, you hung right in there with him for the whole three rounds," Billy replied.

"But he knocked me out!"

"Knockout didn't count, though," Tubbo interjected. "Bell rang at the count of eight, so you got saved by the bell."

The boys had an argument over whether you could be saved by the bell in the final round, with nearly everyone siding against Brain. Little Buck said that it didn't matter, but, deep inside, he was enormously pleased that the official ruling was that he had gone three rounds with Brain, that he had been knocked down only once, and that everyone said he had held his own.

When he returned home, he entered through the side door and went directly upstairs to his room, calling to his mother and grandmother in the kitchen, "Hi, I've got some work to do in my room."

Afraid to let anyone see his bloodied, battered face, yet too tired to stay on his feet, Little Buck pulled a pillow and blanket from his bed and huddled in the corner of his bedroom closet. Although his body shook with chills and his ribs ached each time he took a breath, he soon lapsed into a deep sleep. In his troubled dreams, the garage spun crazily around, the ropes ensnared his arms as a huge gorilla wearing boxing gloves, but with Brain's discolored head set upon its shoulders, repeatedly smashed his face and then tore his left arm from its socket. Tossing and sweating beneath the blanket in the dark, stifling closet, Little Buck then dreamed that he was standing behind the home team's bench at the ball field, forlornly watching Steel Valley take the field, except they had no first baseman. The empty left sleeve of his jacket was pinned up, like an armless soldier he had seen. Sitting in the first row of the bleachers, shaking his head disgustedly, was Big Buck. He could hear his grandfather telling the men around him what a great first baseman Little Buck could have been if only he hadn't fought Brain.

Then he felt someone shaking his arm as his grandfather's voice got louder, "What in the world have you been into, kiddo?"

Blinking, he opened his eyes and saw Big Buck standing in the doorway, with Little Buck's mother and grandmother behind him.

"What have you been into?" Big Buck repeated, as Little Buck's mother pushed passed her father to throw her arms around her son.

"Little Buck, what's happened to you?" she cried out.

"Oh, my God, someone's given him a terrible beating. Let's get the police!" his grandmother shrieked.

"Slow down, Victoria," Big Buck said as he lifted his grandson out of the closet and laid him on the bed. "Now, what happened, kiddo?"

Little Buck tried not to cry as he told them of the boxing match in Brain's garage, while his mother helped him out of his clothes, gently washed his face, and slipped on his pajamas. His grandmother still wanted to call the police, but Big Buck said that would be ridiculous. She then said that she was going directly to Brain's house to give him and his parents a piece of her mind. And she would have, if Big Buck had not stopped her.

"Listen, Victoria, you're absolutely right that a sixteen-year-old boy shouldn't be fighting an eleven-year-old, but if I heard Little Buck right, he challenged the Conlon boy. Isn't that so, Little Buck?"

Sitting on the edge of his bed as his mother wrapped another blanket around him, Little Buck sighed and nodded.

"Now, that was a dumb thing to do," Big Buck said, jiggling his grandson's hand. "It's not your style to get in over your head, to start something you can't finish, to make a rash decision with the seat of your pants instead of your head. Is it, kiddo?"

Staring down at the floor, Little Buck shook his head, dejectedly, as his mother hugged him, and his grandmother stood glaring through the window in the direction of the Conlon home.

"Now, pay attention, Victoria," Big Buck said, turning to his wife. "I don't want you saying a word about this to the Conlons or anyone else. It'll just make matters worse. Word will spread around the block that Little Buck's a Mamma's boy, or, worse still, a Grandma's boy. If anyone mentions it we just shrug and say that Little Buck's got to learn to take care of himself. Understand, Victoria?"

"Oh, I suppose, if you say so, Joseph."

"Mercy?"

"If you think it's best, Dad."

* * * * * *

Walking past Brain's garage, Little Buck pressed his thumb against his cheek, recalling the summer afternoon when only he, among the younger boys, had mustered up the courage to stand up to Brain, to go the whole three rounds with only him being knocked down once. And then he remembered his grandmother wanting to storm into the Conlon home, to chastise them for letting such a fight occur. Only Big Buck could have stopped her, he thought. Now, who's going to stop her, he wondered. Who's going to keep her from turning me into a little Lord Fauntleroy, now that Big Buck's gone?

Chapter Seven

Nothing's the Same

Stopping at the corner, he nearly turned around and went back home. Maybe I can get Nan to trim my hair again, he thought. Hesitating, he recalled his mother's comment that Big Buck would be ashamed of his straggly hair, so he trudged on, trying to take his mind off the agonizing confrontation that lay ahead.

Maybe I'll get called out Monday, he thought. The coach obviously picked Tubbo for the line, so that gives me a better chance. Who cares anyway, he shrugged. Seventh graders hardly ever get to play. Maybe I won't bother, even if they put my name on the board. But then, people would say I was scared. What would Big Buck say? Baseball's our sport, anyway. Cripes, I wish he were here!

Crossing into the next block, realizing that he only had another block to go, he looked across the street to the old Hart home. Only Emily lived there now. She was Rip's sister, and Big Buck's niece. She's almost as kind as Mom, Little Buck thought. Yet, there was much more to her than that. She was different from the other women of Steel Valley. She led the most exciting life in town, maybe even more exciting than starring in all three sports.

After her father, Great Uncle John, had died, in the depths of the Depression, Emily had quit school at age fifteen. Fibbing about her age to get a job, as a clerk in Nathan's Shoe Store in nearby Coalton, she had rapidly become the top salesman in the store. Not a clerk, but a salesman. She liked to tell how Harry Nathan emphasized that he had many clerks but few salesmen, and that according to him, she had the natural gift.

"Customers want three things," she stressed to Little Buck, "a smile, a clean store, and value for their money."

Emily knew all the tricks of the trade, too. "First thing, always remove the customer's shoe and slip it out of sight behind his chair. You don't want him leaving while you're in the stock room. Never keep more than two pairs of shoes in front of the customer. It will confuse him. Sometimes, after you've shown him several pairs, you might even be able to sell him the first or second pair that he previously rejected. If you can't make a sale, always turn the customer over to the manager before he gets his shoe back on. Never tell a woman her shoe size unless she insists. If you don't have the right size, try a longer and narrower size or a shorter and wider size but never, never ever misfit a child!" That was Harry Nathan's cardinal rule. People in the valley knew it, too. That's probably why he was so successful.

Once when Little Buck's mother had taken him to Nathan's for shoes, Harry Nathan, himself, had told them, "Why that Emily Hart was the best shoe salesman I ever had!" That was after Emily had moved on to the shoe department at Gimbel's in Pittsburgh. By twenty-one, she was a section head; by twenty-three, an assistant buyer; and by twenty-six, a full-fledged buyer, flying to New York City several times a year.

Little Buck loved to sit beside Emily on the floor in front of her living room fireplace on winter evenings, shaking her long-handled popcorn maker over the flickering flames, listening to her describe the excitement of her job, and her trips to New York City.

She had the habit of smiling and nodding affirmatively when she spoke. One evening, she confided to Little Buck that it was a habit that she had worked very hard to cultivate.

"If you want to be a persuader, Little Buck, you've got to get people to begin responding unconsciously to little suggestions. A smile will help people begin to like you, and before they know it, they'll be shaking their heads right along with you." Then, as she talked, she stretched her arms out and yawned. Within a few seconds Little Buck yawned, too.

"See that!" she laughed, pointing at Little Buck's mouth. "You unconsciously responded to my yawn by yawning yourself. That's the power of suggestion, Little Buck. Never forget it!"

No wonder Emily was so successful, Little Buck thought. Just like Harry Nathan had said, she had the natural gift. She could charm a gruff old steelworker. Yet, she wasn't exactly pretty. She was tall, and skinny as a rail. Her nose was too big for her face, a lot like her brother, Rip's. But his nose had been broken three times. Little Buck decided that Emily made the most of what she had. Every strand of her long blond hair was immaculately in place, turned up slightly at the ends like June Allison's. Unlike the other women in town, she seldom wore dresses, but rather perfectly pleated skirts with frilly white blouses and jackets that always matched the skirts. Little Buck was certain that when Emily got into a taxi at LaGuardia Airport, with her real leather briefcase under her arm, the cabbie just naturally assumed that she was one of those high-powered buyers coming to their city, the most important city in the world, to make million dollar decisions that would help set the style for millions of Americans in the coming seasons. And, of course, she was.

Most people didn't appreciate how difficult it was to be a buyer for a big department store. When people went to buy their Easter shoes, they didn't realize that the buyer had to make their spring selections before Thanksgiving. Or when mothers picked out their children's back-to-school shoes, they never thought about the poor buyer who had to order them right after Easter. It was a terribly risky business. If you guessed wrong, you could cost the store thousands of dollars, and end up without a job. But Emily didn't guess. She kept meticulous records of what sold well the previous seasons, and on her lunch hour she browsed through the other stores in town, and on the weekends she studied stacks of fashion magazines. Before the war, she even subscribed to a magazine that came all the way from Paris. Although she couldn't read French, she studied the pictures, even pasting some of them up on her dresser mirror. She always tried to arrive in New York on the weekend before her buying trip began, so she could investigate the latest fashions in the stores along Fifth Avenue and tour all the important sights. With her own eyes, she had seen the Statue of Liberty, the Empire State Building and Radio City Music Hall! And she never went to New York without bringing back a gift for Little Buck. Best of all, he liked a hand-carved wooden statue of old peg-legged Peter Stuyvesant and Washington Irving's book about the headless horseman.

Little Buck decided that if he ever had to have a girlfriend, he would want her to be like Emily, even though that probably wouldn't sit too well with Nan. Realizing Emily would not be home from work until late Saturday evening, he knew he was welcome to help himself to the lemon cookies in the jar on top of her icebox. Anyway, he was in no hurry to get his haircut. Taking a bottle of milk from her front porch and walking around to her back door, he unearthed a key from her flowerpot and entered the house.

After putting the milk in the icebox, pouring himself a glass from an opened bottle, and setting the jar of lemon cookies on the oilcloth-covered table, he collapsed onto a kitchen chair in front of them. Glumly, he unscrewed the lid, removed a lemon cookie, and dunked it in his milk. Why couldn't his life be exciting like Emily's, he brooded. She had made something of herself. She had gone beyond their valley, and that was what Big Buck kept saying Little Buck should do.

As he dunked another cookie, it crumbled into soggy bits. Disgusted with himself, he emptied the glass into the sink, mumbling, "But she knows practically everything, and I can't even dunk my cookie right." Nearly in tears, he listlessly rinsed his glass and returned it to Emily's cupboard. Locking the door and returning the key to the flowerpot, he stood dejectedly, staring into the alley. What's left for me, he wondered, now that Big Buck's gone?

Resuming his hated trip to the barber shop, Little Buck thought about Cousin Emily's success, about her brother, Rip, making a name for himself in an entirely different way, about the excitement on the block over Tubbo Grimes being called out for football, and the good possibility that his name would be on Monday's blackboard, too. But none of that seemed to matter anymore. All he could think of was the dreaded moment when he would enter his grandfather's shop. What should he say to the new barber? What would it be like, just being another customer, sitting on one of the hard-backed wooden chairs waiting his turn?

Approaching the town's main intersection, he paused at the corner, leaned against a telephone pole, and stared across the street at the three-story stone building. Like a granite rock surrounded by sticks of driftwood, it dominated the street, and governed the lives of the town's inhabitants, clutching tight behind its ponderous doors the wealth of the community, the mortgages on their homes, and the dollars that it doled out reluctantly in exchange for notes that tied the people to their town and to the mill behind it. The bank seemed to stand guard jealously over the main entrance to the mill, waiting to snatch their checks from the men as they emerged on payday, watching to extract its measure from the wealth produced among the fumes and clangor behind the gates. Even though the bank and mill were in the bottom of the river valley, bracketed by an inhabited hillside on the east and a sheer cliff on the west, the bank and the mill, rather than the higher elevations, commanded everything in sight. Our world's turned upside down, Little Buck remembered his grandfather's comment, as he studied the bank and its surroundings.

Chiseled above the iron doors was the name "Steel Valley National Bank." On the second floor of this building were doctors' offices and the law office of Angustus Felton, which also served as his local congressional office. On the third floor was the headquarters for the draft board. People spoke in hushed voices when they referred to it. Beneath the bank, in the basement, was the barber shop. The bank could have been any bank. The doctors' offices could have been any doctors' offices. And the lawyer-congressman's office could have been any lawyer-congressman's office. But the barber shop was like no other.

It was a turn-of-the-century, pure Norman Rockwell painting. Especially when it was filled with customers: mill hands, shopkeepers, and a professional man or two clustered around the pot-bellied stove or shifting about on the hard wooden chairs along the back wall, engaged in easy conversation, waiting their turn while Big Buck draped a candy-striped sheet over one of their neighbors, lathered and cranked him back for a straight razor shave.

Three giant hand-pumped Kokin barber chairs faced a mirrored wall that was framed with intricate gingerbread oak carvings. Beneath the mirror ran a long marble counter housing three sinks with ornate brass spigots and an assortment of combs, brushes, razors, hair tonics, shaving lotions and powders. A

dozen long leather razor straps hung evenly along the
counter ledge. On the wall between the mirror and
street window wells hung a honeycomb of cubbyholes
filled with hand-painted shaving mugs. Beneath the
window wells, along the front wall facing the street,
or, more accurately, facing the grated hole under the
street, perched a shoeshine stand. It seemed odd to
Little Buck that windows facing concrete shafts beneath the street should be adorned with lace curtains
and potted plants, but Nan regularly washed the curtains and Big Buck tended to the plants himself. In the
center of the ceiling a copper-plated fan spun lazily,
occasionally wafting a clip of hair across the eggshell
white tiled floor. The creamy walls and ceiling, painted
annually on Easter Monday, made the underground
quarters seem larger than they were. And the bright-
ness provided the necessary light for an artist at his
work. And, of course, that's what Big Buck was: an
artist who sculpted hair, and shaped faces through his
shaves and mustache trims. Even grimy millhands expected custom cuts that enhanced their best features,
hid a cowlick or made big ears small. And he never let
them down.

Only the center barber chair was now used, but in
the early years, Big Buck's brother, Bob, had used the
chair on the right, and Mac had used the other chair
when he was learning his trade. How I wish I could have
been there with them, Little Buck thought, leaning
against the telephone pole, studying his grandfather's
shop from across the street. He could see himself shining shoes on Saturday nights, his arms aching, as customers occupied all fourteen chairs around the wall,
with the overflow standing at the stove, or lounging
on the rail outside in summertime.

Glancing at Mac's shop, a few doors up the street,
he recalled walking past Mac's, peering through the window, counting only three cheap, plastic-covered, un-
matched chairs. Kitchen rejects! Yet, Big Buck seldom

had more than two or three customers waiting during all the years Little Buck could remember. He looked from Mac's shop across the street to the bank, measuring the distance. He was standing closer to Mac's than to his grandfather's shop.

Then he noticed Rube Parnham sitting in his regular spot on the bank steps, motioning to him. It wasn't yet noon, and already Rube looked soused, like he had slept in his grimy pants and tattered shirt. He probably had. His feet were so swollen that he had to cut the tops out of his shoes. He appeared to have difficulty balancing his huge head and blotchy face atop his long lean body. It was hard to believe that he had pitched the Baltimore Orioles to seven consecutive pennants in the 1920s. Big Buck said that he had a 33 and 7 record in 1923. Rube had promised to show Little Buck how to throw a screwball, claiming it was a left-hander's pitch, but he never had. He just sat on the bank steps all day, shuffling back and forth to Bender's Bar, mooching drinks. He was both the town celebrity and the town drunk. How could such a thing happen, Little Buck wondered. Seeing Rube gave him a queasy feeling. Making it to the major leagues had to be any boy's ultimate dream, yet the only major leaguer he actually knew was nothing but a disheveled drunk.

Crossing the street, the boy spoke, "Morning, Rube. Feeling any better today?"

"About the same, Bucko. Sorry about your grandpap. He was always good to me, even though he'd never let me sit on his railing," Rube chuckled. "Where you been hiding?"

"Oh, I've been around."

"Don't forget, next spring I'm going to show you how to throw a screwball."

"I was just wondering, Rube," Little Buck squinted at the gaunt has-been, "with you being right-handed, how can you show me?"

"Why, that don't make no difference. Lefty Grove gave me lots of pointers when I first came up."

"Well, I'm going to hold you to your promise!" Little Buck waved as he walked around the side of the bank to the basement steps, glad to get away from something he didn't understand.

The concrete steps, with their concave surfaces, were worn from nearly half a century of use, from the men of Steel Valley bounding down them to have Big Buck brighten their day, when they emerged thirty minutes later smelling of lilac scent, with each hair trimmed neatly in its place. Descending the steps, Little Buck stomped on the dirt in a corner, and then ran his finger along the bottom of the soot-covered window. What would Big Buck say about that? What would Harry Nathan say about that?

Entering the shop, he was appalled by the footprints and hair clippings on the floor. Nodding to the barber, he sat on a chair alongside two other waiting patrons.

"Ain't you Buck's boy?" the barber asked, glancing at him as he continued cutting hair.

"His grandson," Little Buck replied.

"You mean you haven't met Little Buck?" one of the customers asked. "Why, he's one heck of a shoeshiner."

"So I heard. Been meaning to get in touch with you, boy. How would you like to work for me on Saturdays?"

Looking at the dust-covered shoeshine chair and the tobacco-splotched spittoon, Little Buck replied, "Aw, I don't know. I'd have to ask my Mom." The second the words were spoken, he hated himself for saying that he would have to ask for his mother's permission, even though he knew it was only an excuse.

"You do that, boy, and let me know."

"I'll see," Little Buck mumbled, knowing he had no intention of working for such an impostor. Surveying the shop, he noticed speckles of dried shaving cream

on the center mirror, and cobwebs in the ceiling corner, adjacent to the alcove where Big Buck ate his lunch.
Cobwebs! Big Buck would turn over in his grave if he
could see his shop. Especially on a Saturday morning,
we would have had the whole place spic and span clean
before Big Buck raised the blind, as he squirmed around
on the hard chair. But I sure don't miss cleaning out
the spittoon, he thought, nearly gagging at the sight
of it.

When his turn came and he climbed into the chair,
the barber threw a wrinkled sheet over him without
even first wrapping a tissue around his neck.

"Want it cut short, boy?" the barber asked, reek-
ing of tobacco juice, his teeth discolored and stained.

"Regular will do."

For the next fifteen minutes, neither the barber
nor the boy spoke. The odor of stale cigarette smoke
and tobacco juice hung in the air that once had smelled
of Noxema and lilac scent. The waiting patrons shifted
restlessly without any pleasant conversation from the
barber to help them pass the time. Already, the magazines were dog-eared and out of date, and the *Post
Gazette* was nowhere in sight. How could you get the
box scores without the morning paper?

This fellow won't last long, Little Buck concluded.
No personality...no Sen-Sen to cover up his bad
breath...and a dirty shop! Why, if this was my first time
at Big Buck's, he already would know how old I was,
what sports I played, what I thought about Steel Valley's
chances this fall, and a whole lot more.

The noon whistle sounded, and Little Buck's mind
drifted to the mill, imagining the men commencing
their staggered, twenty-minute lunch breaks. The con-
tents of their black lunch pails were pretty much alike
with baloney or salami sandwiches plastered with
mustard or catsup, a hard-boiled egg, a few pieces of
fruit, a slice of cake or pie, and a thermos of ice coffee
or tea. Some carried beer or wine in their thermos,

but that was a good way to lose an arm, or get docked a full day's pay. Regardless of what the men on the coke ovens carried in their buckets, by noon it tasted like rotten eggs.

Sometimes, workers on the first trick would stop in the barber shop after work, still sweat-soaked, and caked with lime and coal dust. Little Buck had studied them on summer afternoons during shift changes, the men shuffling toward the mill, already seemingly exhausted. But the workers, leaving the mill after eight hours of heavy labor in one hundred degree temperatures, would burst through the gate, laughing, swinging their lunch buckets, some even trotting. How could that be, he wondered.

He was puzzled that the white and colored workers seemed to separate into two groups as they fanned out through the narrow mill gate, even though they had been working side by side all day long. Occasionally, he would overhear some of the white mill hands poking fun at the colored workers behind their backs, or mimicking the way they talked. He couldn't understand why people said, "The colored should be kept in their place," and why they had to live in a cluster of dilapidated houses up the hollow on the edge of town. They seemed like hardworking decent people to him. Some of the school's best athletes came from the hollow, and Morris Washington had written the school poem for the senior yearbook. Big Buck never said anything bad about them, but then, he never cut their hair either.

He had noticed that most of the older mill workers had a deep, wheezing cough, which Nan had blamed on smoking. But Big Buck had said it was silicosis—white lung—caused by breathing the ore and lime dust in the mill.

Occasionally, sitting on the bank steps with Rube Parnham, he would watch the men entering Bender's Bar to down a few boilermakers. He supposed that was all right after a hard day's work, even though Big Buck said that eventually it would eat out your insides. Little Buck decided that boilermakers wouldn't be his style. What he couldn't understand were the men who stopped at Bender's for boilermakers before their shifts began. Big Buck had said, "If you had to spend your life in that damn inferno, you might want to get pickled before you went in, too. Which is one more reason for staying out of the mill, kiddo!"

Big Buck had instilled in him a fear of working in the mill. Not a physical fear, although there was reason enough for that, but rather a fear that if he once walked through the gate, if he worked there for just one day, he would be ruined for life. The big money—nearly $3 an hour, more than workers could earn anywhere else—would hook him forever, as it did most of the young men before the war. Never mind the layoffs and the strikes. When they were called back, they all went. They knew nothing else. And with the babies and the bills, they had no choice.

Since the war began, the mill was working three shifts a day, seven days a week. Nothing could stop the incessant clanging of steel being pounded into shape, of smoke belching from the high smokestacks, of the sky suddenly blazing afire, as though the world were coming to an end when one of the blast furnaces was tapped. The smoke and soot mingled with fog which formed a dense smog that hung in the valley until nearly noon, each day. Sometimes on rainy days it remained, blanketing the town like a shroud, making tempers flair and dispositions sour. Worst of all, were windy Monday afternoons when the mill set off the quencher. As hopper cars of red-hot coke rolled down from the ovens and under the huge enclosed water tower, the cold water dousing the glaring coals produced a soot cloud shooting through the tower into the sky. If the wind blew any direction but west—and it seldom blew west due to the high cliff on the other side of the river—the gargantuan soot cloud usually descended within a half mile of the quencher, showering black particles, the size of snowflakes, down upon hundreds of washes strung out on clothes lines in the back yards of the valley.

Following a solemn meeting with the town's Protestant and Catholic clergy which was one of the few times they united on anything, the mill agreed to sound its whistle on Monday afternoons before setting off the quencher. When that happened, women would scurry out of their homes, like volunteer firemen racing for the firehouse, into their back yards frantically gathering their laundry, white sheets first, to escape the discharge from the monster.

The mill whistle had other meanings, too. It defined their days, sounding every shift change: at seven in the morning, three in the afternoon, and eleven at night, even at Christmas and Easter. It woke you in the morning, told you when school was nearly over, and when everyone should be in bed.

Its three shrill blasts meant someone had been hurt. Then, the whole town froze, waiting for the wail of the ambulance siren. People came out of the stores on Main Avenue, standing along the curb, hoping for a glimpse of the victim as the ambulance sped by. Wives and mothers dropped their housework and ran to their front porch steps, waiting for word to be passed along the avenue. Some would even run along the street toward the mill, untying their aprons as they went, praying that it was not their husband, son or father in the ambulance. And then, as an afterthought, praying for all their neighbors, too.

Two types of injuries occurring most frequently were burns from splashing molten steel when the blast furnaces or open hearths were tapped, and blows from falling ingots as they moved along the mill. The Presbyterian preacher always gave thanks at his New Year's sermon if the mill had made it through the year without any fatalities.

Nearly everyone hated the mill, despising how it consumed their lives just as it devoured the necessary quantities of coke, limestone and iron ore into its blast furnaces each day. Yet, their lives were totally dependent on it. When the mill shut down, the whole town suffered because there was no money for clothes, not enough food, and many of the rowhouses on the hill were heated only by coal scavenged from along the railroad tracks.

Sitting in the barber chair, studying the lined, grimy faces of the two waiting customers, Little Buck wondered how people could loathe the mill, yet love the town that existed because of it. No one ever even considered moving somewhere else. Steel Valley was their home. It was where they belonged. It was where most of them were born, would work, raise a family and die. Yet, many of the old folks on the hill had emigrated from Poland, Italy, or Czechoslovakia. Why would it be unthinkable for their children or grandchildren to move away from Steel Valley? Little Buck wished that he had thought to ask Big Buck that question.

When the barber finished, he didn't bother to brush Little Buck's neck with talcum powder, or hold up a mirror so the boy could inspect the back of his head. When Little Buck paid him, the barber just grunted and asked, "You'll let me know about working on Saturdays?"

"I'll let you know if I can do it," he replied evasively, turning sideways to see the back of his head in the mirror.

"Steps," he muttered, observing the crude, sharply defined layers of his hair. He was disgusted that there was not the slightest shaping, none of the fine sculpting that typified his grandfather's haircuts.

"What say?" the barber asked.

"Nothing," Little Buck replied, thinking: This is my last haircut here. When Nan sees this, maybe even she'll agree. Maybe next time I can go to Mac's.

Chapter Eight
Everything's Wrong

The following Monday morning, Little Buck's name was posted on the bulletin board along with Tubbo Grimes and Greeky Karris. Everyone crowded around him, slapping him on the back, telling him how lucky he was. But he didn't feel any of their excitement. He just shrugged, "Suppose I'll go down to the locker room after school. Got nothing else to do."

The hand-me-down uniform they gave him was three sizes too big. The padded knees of the torn and taped pants nearly touched his ankles, and the shoulder pads rubbed against his elbows when he did his side bends. Stuffing cotton into the toes of his high topped, cleated shoes, and a sponge into the interior webbing of his battered helmet, he practiced each day with the scrubs, usually as a defensive safety against the ninth graders who easily overran the younger boys. Among the seventh and eighth graders, only Tubbo Grimes was able to hold his ground on the line against the first team, and only Little Buck was able to keep up with them when the team ran their laps. But the coach didn't seem to notice. During the first week, Little Buck never got to carry the ball, never got to run a single play on offense.

Sitting dejectedly in class on Friday afternoon, waiting for early dismissal so he could get suited up for their first game, he felt like crying as he imagined how foolish he was going to look running onto the field in his ragged, ill-fitting practice uniform. Only his shirt would be different. For games, the scrubs were given faded senior high shirts, red with white letters, which meant that his game shirt undoubtedly would be too big. The game was only two hours away, and he still didn't even know his number. Big deal, he thought. Staring through the window at a white oak tree, he wondered if the acorns had begun to fall, but couldn't tell from where he sat. Digging into the pocket of his corduroy knickers, he extracted two shriveled, moldy buckeyes. Jiggling them together in his hand underneath his desk, he glumly studied them. Why haven't the new buckeyes started dropping? Everything's gone wrong since Big Buck died! The taste of eraser dust clogged his throat, and the smell of the recently oiled wooden floor filled his nostrils.

Miss Baker was droning on, describing the Mediterranean and how it helped shape the civilization surrounding it. Who cares? Little Buck thought, looking at the clock above a picture of George Washington. Taking his penknife, he flicked open the small blade and lightly jabbed the neck of the girl in front of him.

As Rebecca Hall squealed, Miss Baker's eyes peered in her direction. "Rebecca, what's wrong?"

"Nothing...nothing, Miss Baker. I...I think a mosquito bit me," she stammered, rubbing her neck.

"Mosquitoes after Labor Day? Hmmpf...," Miss Baker slapped her pointer across her hand and she clomped down the aisle toward Little Buck.

"Did you see a mosquito, Joseph?"

"No, ma'am."

"Did you pinch Rebecca, Joseph?"

"No, ma'am."

"What do you think caused her to squeal like that, Joseph?"

Furrowing his eyebrows and shaking his head as he looked up, wide-eyed, at Miss Baker, Little Buck replied, "I guess *something* must have made her jump."

The boys in the room snickered and the girls giggled as Little Buck's big blue eyes stared, unblinking, at the teacher. Her eyes narrowed into slits as she studied his face, and then turned abruptly, stomping toward the blackboard to resume her lecture on the Mediterranean in an agitated, clipped voice, smacking the blackboard with the tip of her pointer to identify ancient Thebes on the map she had drawn.

"College heels," Little Buck muttered under his breath, sizing up his new teacher. She glanced in his direction, but he smiled angelicly at her, thinking: College heels...what's Emily say about them? Oh, yes...means she cares more about how her feet feel than how they look. Bet she's going to be a tough old bird!

The last half hour before the early dismissal for the three seventh-grade celebrities dragged on. For Little Buck, since his grandfather's death, every hour of every day seemed to hang suspended, barely grinding on, in an empty grayish void. Nothing mattered anymore: not the joy of starting a new school year, or of moving from grade school to junior high; not the thrill of being called out for football; not the anticipation of Steel Valley's new football season; not the exhilaration of the pennant race; not the enervating trepidation that accompanied their planning for fall garden raids; not the excitement of gathering around the radio for FDR's fireside chats; nor the news of bombing raids on Berlin, or the bloody capture of another island in the Pacific. Life had lost its savor.

Later in the locker room, when the coach winked at him as he tossed him jersey number twenty-two, Little Buck tried to smile. That was Rip's old number; maybe even the very same jersey Rip had worn. When people saw him wearing twenty-two, they would automatically associate him with his famous cousin and expect him to be as good, except they probably would laugh when they saw how foolish he looked—like Snoopy, or Dopey, or even Grumpy.

"Damn," he muttered, stuffing his shirttail into his pants nearly covering his knees.

Sitting on the end of the bench with the rest of the scrubs, Little Buck watched the first team run over Mon Junction, almost as easily as they had destroyed the scrubs.

Glancing over his shoulder, he saw his mother, sitting alone, in the bleachers. She smiled and waved at him even though he pretended not to see her. She walked here just to see me sitting on the bench, he thought, grinding his cleats into the dirt. What'd she do that for?

By half time, Steel Valley Junior High was ahead, twenty-one to zero. As the coach outlined their game plan for the second half and told the second team to warm up, Little Buck thought: Maybe I'll get in...maybe the scrubs will get to play. Returning to the bench for the beginning of the second half, he felt an empty queasiness in the pit of his stomach. His arms seemed light and numb, and his chest tightened as he worried: What if I screw up when they put me in the game? That Mon Junction fullback must have thirty pounds on me. What if he runs right over me? Even worse, what if I duck when he comes at me? What if I don't hit him square?

Then he remembered Big Buck's advice: "Don't you be trying to make square, head-on tackles. That's for bigger boys, the linebackers and the horses on the line. You hit 'em low...go for the ankles. Use your speed and leverage. Makes no difference where you're coming from—in front of him, beside him, or behind him— go for his ankles."

Taking a deep breath, Little Buck muttered, "Go for the ankles."

"What?" asked Tubbo Grimes, who was sitting next to him.

"Nothing. Watch the game. I think we're going to get in," Little Buck replied, peering intently at the cloud of dust enveloping the players on the field.

At the start of the fourth quarter, when Steel Valley was ahead, thirty-four to zero, the coach put in the second team.

"We'll get in about halfway through the quarter, unless the Junction scores a couple of touchdowns," Little Buck whispered to Tubbo.

When the midpoint of the last quarter came, the scrubs were still sitting on the bench. Mon Junction had scored one touchdown, and Steel Valley's second team had been unable to move the ball.

With two minutes left in the game and Mon Junction in a punting situation, Steel Valley called a time-out, and the coach turned to the scrubs: "All right, third team, get out there to receive the punt, then go on offense. Only running plays, Kachurik," he called to the eighth grade quarterback, clapping his hands.

"Who should go back for the punt?" Kachurik shouted, running backwards onto the field.

Hesitating, the coach scanned the scrubs, then cupping his hands, yelled back, "Helwig!"

Little Buck's legs nearly buckled when he heard his name. Protesting in the huddle that he had never practiced catching punts, although he had done it often in pick-up games in the vacant lot next to old Man Schmidt's, Kachurik elbowed him in the ribs. "Shut up Helwig! One man back for the punt. That's you, Helwig. Take it down the right sideline. The rest of you guys, block left."

Standing on his own thirty yard line, his stomach churning wildly, Little Buck tried to dry his clammy hands on his jersey as he bent forward, squinting toward the punter. Each time he tried to take a deep breath, he thought his chest would explode.

The kick was short and wobbly. Little Buck ran forward about ten yards, then realizing he had misjudged it, started backpedaling. The ball seemed to be plummeting toward him as his helmet tilted down across his eyes. As the ball smacked his chest, a tackler's shoulder pads smashed into his stomach. The ball popped out of his arms as his body crashed into the dust. A swarm of Mon Junction players pounced on the ball as Little Buck lay crumpled, gasping for breath. As his teammates helped him off the field, he saw his mother start down out of the stands toward him and then stop on the bottom bleacher, clutching her handkerchief.

"Oh, *please* don't come down here," he muttered to himself, dreading the further humiliation of her presence on the field.

Shaking his head disgustingly, the coach turned his back on Little Buck as he stumbled toward the bench. Although several of his teammates tried to console him, patting his shoulder or slapping his knee, he hung his head in disgrace. He would never be a football player. He could never live up to his cousin, Rip. Thank goodness Big Buck wasn't there to see him make such a fool of himself.

That weekend, he stayed in his room, except at mealtimes, even though his chums came to the door several times looking for him to come out and play. He rearranged his baseball cards, studying the players statistics, even though he knew most of them by heart. He rummaged through his toy box, stuffing most of them in the garbage can at the end of the backyard, except for a miniature iron truck which Big Buck had given him, and a pearl-handled Gene Autry pistol which he slipped under the pillow of his bed. He should have gotten rid of his toys long ago, especially his old Raggedy Andy doll. He would have to be more grownup now that Big Buck was gone. Sitting at his bedroom window, staring at the two buckeye trees, he fretted at the lateness of their dropping. I could shake them down with a clothesline pole, he thought. But Big Buck said we shouldn't rush them. They'll drop when they're ready. Everything in its own time. "Damn, I wish they'd fall," he muttered aloud. "Things might be all right again if I could just get us our double buckeyes."

The following week he kept to himself, watching from the living room window each morning, waiting until his chums had started up the street before he left for school. During recess he went to the boy's lavatory, sitting in one of the stalls, reading the *Post Gazette* box scores as the Cardinals and the Yankees battled in their respective leagues to repeat their pennant victories of the previous year. He went to football practice each afternoon, but stood on the sidelines watching, unless the coach gave him a specific order. On Friday morning, he complained of a sore throat to his mother, knowing she would keep him home from school. He had no intention of sitting on the bench for the second game, of being put in during the closing moments after the game was won, and probably making a fool of himself again.

But he had made a terrible miscalculation. He had forgotten about his chocolate milk.

For fifteen cents a week, students could receive a half-pint of white or chocolate milk daily. If you brought a note from home stating you couldn't afford it, you could get your milk free. Most of the children turned in their notes every Monday morning, but that would have been unthinkable for him. He wasn't quite sure why he wouldn't have qualified, especially during the months when the family hadn't been able to make the mortgage payments. But he knew not to ask. Each Monday morning his mother dug into her change purse for his fifteen cents, or if she didn't have it his grandmother produced the coins with her admonition: "You be sure to order white milk. Chocolate's bad for you. It'll give you pimples."

And then, as if her instructions had not been sufficiently clear, or he had possibly forgotten them, she brought up the subject again at the dinner table that evening. "Little Buck, did you order white milk today?"

"I'm not crazy. I don't want a face full of pimples," he replied, evasively.

The truth was, he hated the taste of white milk. He never ordered it. Chocolate was his style.

After school, on the day he feigned his sore throat, Mary Beth Grimes, Tubbo's sister, came knocking on the door. The instant Little Buck heard her voice, he knew he was in big trouble.

"Here's Little Buck's milk, Mrs. Hart. I brought him a straw, too. Tell him I hope he feels better soon."

"Darn her anyway," he thought, as he lay on the living room couch where his mother had insisted he stay. "And why did Nan have to answer the door?" he cringed. "Nothing's going right!"

Within seconds, his grandmother was standing over him, with the bottle of chocolate milk in her hand. "So, you've been drinking chocolate milk! I sensed as much. What are we going to do with you, Joseph? Lying to us...."

"I never lied about it. I hate white milk. It makes me want to puke!"

"You never lied to us? You never promised to order white milk?"

"Never. I just said I'd be crazy to order chocolate milk after what you said about pimples. And I'm crazy about chocolate milk. So there!"

"What are we going to do with this boy, Mercy?"

"Oh, Mother, a little chocolate milk won't hurt him. He puts white milk on his cereal every morning. Let's just let him have it today. It might help his sore throat."

"Well, I'm only the boy's grandmother. If you want a pimply-faced son with bad eating habits, that's up to you."

So Little Buck got to sip his half-pint of chocolate milk from the straw that Mary Beth Grimes had provided, on the condition that he would order only white milk in the future. He could easily make the promise, for he had already figured out how he could keep it, yet still get his chocolate milk. He would order white, and then swap with Mary Beth, whom he was certain would cooperate with him.

Although Mary Beth was only ten months younger than her brother, Tubbo, they were in the same grade. She and Little Buck were the youngest in their class. Little Buck often studied Mary Beth and Tubbo, wondering how they could be from the same family. She was a slender, well-groomed, pretty girl with bright blond hair, always neatly trimmed in a pageboy style. She always smelled so fresh, like a shiny new wrapper from a bar of Palmolive soap. She was never sweaty like her brother, and she always spoke in a pleasant, lilting voice, so different from his growls and grunts. And the rounded calves of her shapely little legs looked better than any of the junior high cheerleaders, even though they were two years older. Little Buck liked the special way she treated him, from the time they had entered first grade together. But what he liked best about her was her lips. They were full and soft, and very moist right after she had dabbed on lipstick with her little finger, which she always wiped off on her way home from school. Sometimes when he looked at her, he felt a strange, tingling sensation that he didn't understand. He decided that for a girl, she wasn't half-bad. If only he had asked her to keep his secret.

After school the following Monday, Little Buck explained to the coach that his mother wanted him to skip practice until his throat healed. Not wanting to go home where he probably would be interrogated again about the chocolate milk episode, and afraid to be seen playing on the street with his other chums, Little Buck decided to climb the hill overlooking Steel

Valley. He and Big Buck had done it several times, usually on Sunday afternoons, first ascending the steep cobblestone street past the rundown double-houses of the immigrant mill workers, then winding up the path toward a clump of straggly trees below the crest. The hilltop, itself, was barren. Big Buck had said that the sulfur fumes from the coke ovens had destroyed all the vegetation, that after the mill had come to the valley, the farmers on the hilltop had gotten together and had threatened to sue the steel company, but nothing had come of it.

As Little Buck approached the clump trees below the crest, he turned off the path and edged his way along a ledge to the trees. Pushing back the branches, he peered into an opening in the hillside. Every few feet, rotting timbers braced the walls, and several cross timbers from the shaft's ceiling lay askew against the walls and along the floor. Little Buck could taste the coal dust in his throat as he spit into the abandoned mine. He had asked Big Buck how they had hauled the coal down from the mine, but he hadn't known. The mine had been abandoned before Big Buck had moved to the valley, but he could remember people scavenging coal from the mine in baskets, lugging them down the hill.

Kicking a loose stone from the edge of the precipice, Little Buck watched it fall, bouncing on the path below and rolling to a stop where the path met the cobblestone street. Crouching, he rolled his tongue around his mouth gathering saliva, took a deep breath, and gave a mighty spit over the edge of the cliff. But it flew apart, lost in the wind, before even getting started. Just like my life, he thought, watching the smudge of sun fading behind the smog, hanging over the mill on the cliff across the river. The long, low sheet mill reminded him of a dark scab upon a boney knee. He could smell the sulfur from the coke ovens in the valley.

Flapping out of scrub bushes halfway down the hill, a turkey buzzard ascended toward him, veered off, and disappeared into the smog. The boy felt smothered and alone in the gray stench surrounding him.

"Now I know how Lucky Lindy must have felt above the ocean on his way to France," Little Buck muttered. "Except he was lucky, and my luck's gone." He picked up a small flat stone and sidearmed it off the cliff, nearly losing his balance. My luck disappeared on the day Big Buck died, he thought, and then corrected himself. No, it was on the day he had his stroke. And the proof is that the buckeyes just won't fall. It isn't natural. By mid-September they're always on the ground. How could my life have been so perfect, and then suddenly destroyed? If this is part of growing up, I can do without it. His legs began to ache in his hunkered down position, so he sat down, dangling them over the edge of the cliff, surveying the community below.

It was as though he saw two different towns, separate and apart: One of well-kept homes set back along a tree-lined street, like a tiny, tidy village beneath the Christmas tree; the other of drab, dilapidated, double-houses squeezed into the hillside, like a jumble of faded match boxes. Even the steel mill at the river's edge beneath the sooty vapors of the valley took on an ordered symmetry in contrast to the hodgepodge of houses stuck askew upon the hill.

Yet, the boy reflected, it was the immigrants from the hill who provided the living fuel to keep the factory running, to produce the coke that fired the hated furnaces to turn out the ingots for finishing into useable steel for the other mills throughout their valley. The so-called "better class," living along the valley's floor—the doctors, druggists, lawyers, plant managers and businessmen—was the class that his grandmother insisted included their family, and was totally dependent upon the mill and the men who labored in it. His own father, working as a second helper on the open hearths at Redstone, thirty miles away, was no better than the laborers at Steel Valley, yet it would have been inconceivable to put the family in a class with them. Perhaps that was why Nan was just as happy to have him working so far away.

Little Buck had overheard a conversation between his grandmother and Mr. Hays, the superintendent of the Steel Valley Works, during Big Buck's viewing.

"I was thinking, Mrs. Hart, perhaps we should look into getting your son-in-law transferred closer to home. We probably could find a spot for him on the ovens. It might mean taking third trick, but I believe it could be arranged."

"That's awfully kind of you, Samuel, but best we leave well enough alone for now. We're just thankful that Allan's back to work. He's staying at his mother's and gets home on weekends, so it's really working out quite well."

"Whatever you think."

"I'll speak to him and let you know if he's interested."

Little Buck was certain that she had never mentioned it to his father, and he was thankful that his mother hadn't heard the conversation for it surely would have hurt her deeply. She had confided to Little Buck how much she missed his father, but in the same breath had emphasized that it was a small sacrifice compared to what others were being called upon to make. The boy worried that perhaps he should have told her about the superintendent's offer, but decided it only would have caused more friction in the family. Anyway, he reasoned, it was good that his father could spend some time with Grandma Helwig, who had been living alone for nearly a dozen years since the death of Grandpa Helwig, whom Little Buck had never known.

Shifting back onto his haunches in the cool, gray twilight of a spent September afternoon, he compared the buildings along Main Avenue to the bank, hovering over them all. None came close. Although a few were built of concrete block—both drugstores and the movie house—most were two-story wooden buildings in need of paint. He couldn't tell if the lights were still on in the barber shop beneath the bank. "I couldn't care less," he muttered. He'd never set foot in that place again. His next haircut would be at Mac's. It was his hair! His grandmother didn't need to know. He wondered if the professional men in the offices above the bank had switched their allegiances to Mac. Sooner or later they would. After all, he had learned his trade from Big Buck. And anyone was better than that filthy impostor using Big Buck's shop.

The boy recalled how he had wanted to approach the men upstairs about cleaning their offices during the summer months, but his grandmother had forbidden it.

"You're not some char woman. That's for the Polish women on the hill," she had rebuked him.

Yet, it would have been an easy thing to do, each afternoon after baseball, before Big Buck's closing time. Anything would have been easy compared to cleaning the barber shop spittoon. And, he would have been able to be around the doctors and the lawyers, maybe even around Congressman Felton on Friday afternoons when he usually was in his Steel Valley office.

"Big Buck could have fixed me up with that job easy," the boy muttered. "Now there's no one to help me."

He watched the brightly lit, rickety, old "99" trolley turn the bend at the ball field and begin its trip through town, and then on to Coalton. Why do we always have to ride the trolley when everyone else has a car? It was so embarrassing. His grandmother claimed they didn't need a car because everything was within walking distance. But that wasn't true. His father had to take the train back and forth to Redstone, his mother and grandmother rode the trolley when they did their shopping in Coalton, and Big Buck had to transfer twice when he went to the Guild meetings in Pittsburgh. That was how he and Little Buck always traveled to Pirate baseball games. Those days were gone forever, but he never would forget them. He remembered Big Buck saying that, maybe, some day they would get a car, but even then, he knew the chances were slim. They didn't have the money. Now, there would never be a car; he would spend the rest of his life riding the old "99" to wherever he had to go; and he would spend his life standing in the smog, waiting for a transfer.

Noticing that the trolley had traveled the length of Main Avenue without stopping, he realized that no one was riding it. It was dinner time.

Picking his way down the hill along the shadowed path, he was disheartened that his time alone had produced no satisfactions, no answers to his problems, or insights into how his life should be. When he and Big Buck had climbed the hill, and had stood on the ledge at the mouth of the abandoned coal mine overlooking their valley, he always learned so much, seeing things in a different light, and feeling so good inside. Now, he only felt the same old gnawing emptiness that had engulfed him ever since Big Buck's stroke. Maybe it would never go away.

There was so much he couldn't understand, and, with Big Buck gone, probably never would. Why was it so important that he move to the city after he was grown, when everyone loved their town so much? How could everyone be so loyal to the valley, its schools, its churches, its teams, its neighborhoods, and yet be filled with hatred for the mill that made all those things possible? Why would grown men, even his cousin, Rip, live their lives in the past, as though the most important thing they ever did was play football for Steel Valley High School, or, if they were really good, for the Coalton Olympics? Yet, he felt the same loyalty for the town, and the same excitement about sports. And why would they rarely talk about the war? And why was Emily treated almost like an outcast when she went to church on Sunday just because she had a fancy job in Pittsburgh? He brooded about the town, its people, and why they felt as they did. He worried that he even had such thoughts, and about his inability to find even a glimmer of an answer to any of his questions. He would stumble through life, confused and empty. His life would be one big fumble, like the first punt that he had failed to catch.

When reaching the cobblestone street, he broke into a careful trot, trying to land squarely on each stone so as not to twist his ankles as he descended the dimly lit hill.

Turning onto Oak Avenue, he started running, thinking: It'll be hell to pay if I'm late for dinner.

Emily's was the only unlit house on the block, and passing it, he noticed that her milk was still on her steps. Darn, I should have put her milk in, he thought, but it's too late now. Crossing the street and dashing up the steps to his home, he froze on the front porch. A stranger in a sailor's uniform was standing in their living room. Facing each other, his mother and the stranger were holding hands, laughing and talking animatedly, as his grandmother stood behind them scowling.

Chapter Nine

The Stranger

Slowly turning the front doorknob and softly step-ping into the living room, Little Buck stood mute until they noticed him.

"Hi," he said tentatively, looking from his mother to his grandmother to the stranger in the middle of the room. In his blue bellbottoms and crewcut black hair, the slender young sailor looked taller than his average height.

"Don't tell me this is Little Buck. Why, you were just a baby the last time I saw you."

"Say 'hello' to your cousin, Lawrence," Nan abruptly instructed Little Buck.

Before Little Buck could speak, the sailor grabbed both his arms and shook him enthusiastically. "Look at you. Why, you're the spitting image of your mother."

Wiggling out of the stranger's grasp, Little Buck thought: That's not true. I've got my father's blond hair, and I'm going to look like Big Buck when I grow up. But before he could say anything, his grandmother interceded.

"He's got my widow's peak, Lawrence," she said, reaching over and pushing the boy's hair back above his forehead.

"By golly, Aunt Victoria, I'll say he does."

Naturally, they asked him to stay for supper, which was late that evening due to the excitement of his unannounced appearance.

Lawrence rattled on, explaining that he had en-
listed in the Navy to beat the Army draft, and had
been sent to the Great Lakes Training Center and then
to radioman's school. He proudly displayed the extra
stripe he had gotten upon graduation and a certificate
indicating that he had ranked fourth in a class of 108.
He kept smiling at Mercy and every few minutes reaching over and patting her arm, as though by just looking at her and touching her he was fulfilling a long and
painful hunger.

At least Lawrence's visit had taken Nan's mind off
my being late, Little Buck thought as he sat at the
table studying his new-found cousin.

Nan explained that Lawrence was her deceased
sister Elizabeth's boy, but she didn't seem to want to
talk about that part of the family, so Little Buck just
listened. Lawrence wanted to do most of the talking,
anyway. He told them that he was on his way to San
Diego where he was shipping out with the fleet. He
said he was awful sorry about Big Buck's death; Big
Buck always had been fair with him, although the way
he emphasized Big Buck's name seemed to imply that
someone in the family hadn't treated him right. He
wanted to know all about Little Buck's father, and how
his mother had met him; but most of all, he wanted to
know about her—if, unlike him, she had graduated from
high school; what she had done before getting married; and what were her hobbies. He even wanted to
know her favorite color, and winked at Little Buck after she answered, "Pink." He tried to talk about the
early years when he apparently had spent some time
at the Hart house, but Nan quickly changed the subject, even though it was obvious that those memories
were precious to Little Buck's mother.

They must have been awfully close, once, Little
Buck thought, and then recalling how his mother had
explained that during the early years Mac practically
had been part of the family, turned to the young sailor,

"Did you know Mac, the boy who worked in my grandfather's shop, and learned the trade from Big Buck?"

"Mac...let's see now..."

"Oh, you remember, Larry. He was older than we were. He used to help Dad trim the big hedge out back."

"Sure, I remember him now. He was the fellow who was sweet on you, Mercy. Whatever happened to him?"

"Nothing worthwhile," Nan hissed. "He only set up shop right across the street from us and tried to steal away Buck's trade, after Buck taught him everything he knows."

"Well, sometimes, Aunt Victoria, I guess we end up getting less than we deserve," the young sailor's face hardened as he stared at his aunt.

"Come on, let's go sit in the living room. The dishes can wait," Mercy said, trying to brighten up the conversation.

"Lawrence has to get back to Pittsburgh tonight, so we shouldn't be detaining him," Victoria Hart said as she rose, staring imperiously at her nephew.

"Well, I guess I better be shaking a leg..."

"Oh, Larry, can't you stay for just a little while longer?" Little Buck's mother pleaded, taking hold of his arm.

"Connections are bad this time of night," Nan frowned, adding perfunctorily, "but you're welcome to stay as long as you like, Lawrence."

"Best I be heading out. I've got a long way to go. You look after your mother, Little Buck. She's mighty special to me," he said, tousling the boy's hair, as suddenly the young sailor's eyes filled with tears and he swallowed hard. Quickly turning away from the boy, he pecked his aunt on the cheek.

"I'll write if I can," he mumbled.

"Facing Little Buck's mother, he took both her hands in his and said, smiling through his misty eyes, "Well, looks like it's good-bye again, Mercy. If I don't make it, I wanted you to know that I've named you as my next of kin on my service record, so you'd be my beneficiary..."

"Don't you even be talking like that, Larry. But I love you for it," she squeezed his hands and dashed to the hall closet to get her coat. "I'll walk you to the trolley."

"I'll go with you," Little Buck reached for his baseball cap.

"No! You stay here with me," Nan commanded. "You and I can do the dishes so your mother can walk Lawrence to the trolley," she added, defensively.

Surprised at his grandmother's willingness to wash the dishes, Little Buck shrugged, "Whatever you say, Nan." He could hardly disagree with her when she made it sound like his mother wouldn't be able to walk her cousin to the trolley if he refused to help.

After they had left, as he was rinsing and drying the dishes, he gingerly brought up the subject of his cousin. "How come I never heard of Larry?"

"What's to hear about him? You've got lots of relatives spread across the country. It's just that we're not that close to most of them," his grandmother replied.

"But he and Mom sure seemed close...like they both was all broken up."

"...were, Joseph. It's plural."

"...like they both *were* all broken up about him not being able to stay longer."

"There's no sense in you worrying yourself about things like that. We'll probably never even hear from him again. He's one of those footloose and fancy-free boys without a care or a responsibility. I'm surprised he didn't try to hit us up for some money."

"He seemed pretty serious minded to me."

"Now, what do you know about those kind of things, Little Buck? Take it from me, we're better off without him sniffing around here. He'd only be a burden. The boy's never going to amount to a row of pins. So we had a nice little visit with your long lost relative, and let's just forget about it. You understand, Joseph? You should be thinking about more uplifting things."

"Yes, ma'am," Little Buck replied, not understanding at all, and worrying that there was much more that he should know about Lawrence.

The following afternoon he went to football practice, taking his usual place along the sidelines with the scrubs, except when the coach needed some defensive fodder to feed to the first team.

By Thursday morning, when it was time to order his milk, Little Buck had already made his arrangement with Mary Beth Grimes. Although she had hesitated at first, Little Buck had correctly surmised that he could persuade her to become his co-conspirator.

"Oh, I don't know, Little Buck. Would that be honest?" she had asked.

"You didn't make any promise to my folks, did you?"

"Course not."

"Well, then, you're free to do what you want. Truth is, you'd be helping to keep me honest. You'd be stopping me from lying."

"How's that?"

"Like I told you, I promised them I wouldn't *buy* any chocolate milk. I didn't say I wouldn't *drink* any. So if you won't help me, guess I'll just have to buy it, 'cause white milk makes me gag. You know that. But if you buy chocolate and I buy white, and we swap, then everything's okay. I've kept my word...you don't have me gagging around the playground, maybe even puking on you...and you get your white milk, which is what you want."

"Well, if it will help you, Little Buck, I'll do it!"

"Thanks, Mary Beth, you're a real friend."

"You're not going to the Sock Hop Friday night, are you, Little Buck?"

"Me? I don't go to them things."

"You ought to come sometime. They're lots of fun."

"Me? Go to a dance? You got to be kidding, Mary Beth."

"Well, I just thought you might enjoy it. They have free cookies and punch at intermission."

"Tell you what, if I can get Tubbo interested, we just might stop by for intermission."

Tubbo Grimes, Billy May, Shrimpy Cox, and all the other boys on the block thought that Little Buck had lost his mind when he casually suggested that perhaps they should stop by the junior high Sock Hop on Friday night.

"Get all dressed up to go to a dance? You going soft in the head, Little Buck?" Tubbo had chided him.

"I only meant for the free eats," Little Buck shrugged. "Cripes, I didn't want to go anyway." So that ended that.

By game time on Friday afternoon, he was back into the rhythm of the sport, running laps as fast as the older boys, sweating through his push-ups, and smacking shoulder pads with Tubbo, Greeky, and the other scrubs. But to no avail. Along with his chums, he spent the afternoon on the bench. Steel Valley Junior High won, but only by a touchdown.

It was during the fourth quarter, after he realized that he wouldn't get to play, that he decided to go to Mac's the following morning, regardless of the consequences. Two weeks had passed since his last haircut, and that was time enough. Big Buck always said that a fellow should get his hair cut at least every two weeks if he wanted to look right, so Saturday would be the day. He would even use his own money, taking the coins from his Pennzoil piggy bank. His grandmother couldn't complain about that.

Chapter Ten
A Stunning Revelation

Rising early, while his mother and grandmother still were busy in the kitchen, Little Buck tiptoed down the stairs to the side door. As he went out the door he called back to them, "Got to go to town; I'll be home by noon." Dashing up the sidewalk to get out of earshot before they could reply, he didn't even stop to go through his daily ritual of searching for fallen buckeyes. The plan he had worked out the previous afternoon, while sitting on the bench, included getting to his grandfather's shop before it was open. He could then say he had tried the new barber first, but he wasn't there.

When he arrived at the bank, the blinds were still pulled down on the basement windows, but a light was on. He couldn't remember if the new barber left a light on at night, and feared that he already might be inside. Tiptoeing down the steps, he slowly turned the doorknob, and finding it locked, tiptoed back up the stairs. He had tried. It was already a few minutes past eight on a Saturday morning and the new barber wasn't in the shop!

"He won't last long," Little Buck muttered as he crossed Mac's. The boy pounded on the door but no one answered. He then went next door to the paper store, emptied his pocket of change and moldy buckeyes onto the counter, and after hesitating for a long moment, shrugged, "What the heck." Climbing onto a stool, he ordered a Clark bar and a cherry coke. Thumbing through a *Post Gazette* lying on the counter, he discovered to his chagrin that the sports page was missing, so there was nothing worth reading in the paper. Stuffing the remaining candy bar into his mouth, he drained the coke glass, defiantly sucking the noisy air bubbles through a straw, delighted that his grandmother could not correct him.

Mac walked into the store, bought a paper, turned and left, without seeing Little Buck sitting at the counter. Taking a deep breath, the boy slid off the stool and walked outside. The basement blinds at his grandfather's shop had been raised. The boy hesitated. What would Big Buck want me to do? he wondered. He'd say, "You do what you think is right, kiddo." But how do I know what's right. The boy leaned against the building, and sidearmed a moldy buckeye at a fireplug. He missed. What's right is being close to Big Buck, he told himself...and talking to Mac about Big Buck is a way to get that feeling.

Pushing open the door of Mac's shop, he stepped inside. "Morning, Mac. Looks like I'm your first customer."

"Why, Little Buck Hart! Does your grandmother know you're here?"

"Helwig," the boy corrected him.

"I know your last name, boy. It's just that you'll always be Little Buck Hart to me, and most everyone in town. Don't bother you, me calling you that, does it?"

"Naw," the boy grinned sheepishly, feeling warm and good inside.

"Well, climb up into the chair and let's get at it. My God, boy, somebody put a bowl on your head? Where'd you get this haircut?"

"Across the street at the new barber. Nan said that I should go there since he bought my granddad's stuff. Pretty bad, huh?"

"Awful. Nothing but steps. Big Buck wouldn't let that fellow trim a dog. Course, your grandma has other reasons, too," Mac nodded knowingly as he wrapped a tissue around the boy's neck and draped a candy-striped sheet across his body, pinning at the neck. "Does she know you're here?"

"I get my haircut where I want. I'm paying for this one, anyway."

"Well, your mom and me go way back," the barber said as he snipped away. "Time was when we was like brother and sister."

"She said that you worked for Big Buck, and learned your trade from him."

"Sure did. Never was a better man, neither. Took me off the hill...taught me everything I know."

"What was it like, back then? I guess you were pretty busy, with the shaves and all."

"Oh, they was boom times, no doubt about it. World War I was over. The mill was going three tricks, just like today. The new sheet mill was going up across the river, and people were buying cars. Your grandpap and me was going six days a week, sometimes till midnight on Saturdays."

"I guess you started out like me, shining and cleaning up?"

"Pretty much so. Course, things was different then. Shaving was real big, so I jumped back and forth between lathering and shining. Kept me stepping, I can tell you that."

"How old were you when Big Buck taught you the trade?"

"Well, let's see...I was going on sixteen when he let me cut my pap's and little brother's hair. But I didn't really get into it right until your Uncle Bob left. When your Aunt Nell's mother died and they went to New York, Buck really moved me fast. Needed a second barber quick. He was always a stickler for not keeping fellows waiting. Said you'd start losing customers if you got more than two behind. That's one of the reasons he always kept up such a chatter. He said it made the time pass faster. And he knew everything about everybody. What your kids was up to, how the old folks was fairing, who you liked for the series, how things was going on your trick at the mill. But he'd only talk about the good stuff. Said people didn't want to hear about troubles. Why, he made the fellows feel so good, they'd just hang around the shop to pass the time of day. And they was always welcome, long as they sat in the alcove so people looking down through the windows wouldn't see the chairs all full and think we had a long waiting line."

"How come you left him, Mac?" the boy asked hesitantly.

"Really had no choice, kiddo. When the Depression hit, we didn't have enough work to keep one barber busy. I bummed around for about a year, and then old man McInstry died, leaving the shop standing empty. So my Pap come up with the money for me to get it from McInstry's widow for practically nothing."

"Then you didn't run out on Big Buck?"

"Me run out on your grandfather? After him teaching me the trade? Practically taking me in like I was one of the family? What kind of a person you think I am?"

Little Buck shrugged, watching in the mirror as the barber wet and parted his hair for the final shaping. "I didn't know this was a barber shop before you moved in."

"Where'd you think I'd get the money to buy new equipment? Bad as things was, sometimes I'd go a whole day without a single paying customer. I know it didn't sit too well with Buck, me taking over old man McInstry's, right across the street. But times was hard, and we had to eat. Deep down, Buck understood. But your grandmother...if looks could kill, I'd have been dead about two days after I opened up. She'd even walk up here to get the trolley, instead of catching it right down from your house, so she could stand in front of my shop to see who was inside. Fellows said that she wouldn't even speak to them once she caught them in here. She'd hold her nose up in the air and walk right past them on the street. Some of them was fellows she'd known all her life. Why, she wouldn't even talk to my Uncle Walter. My own uncle! Just because he stopped going to Buck. That grandmother of yours is a dilly," Mac shook his head as his eyes hardened, possibly remembering how she had refused to let him pay his respects before Big Buck's funeral, perhaps recalling the many slights he had endured through the years.

"Big Buck always said we should make allowances," the boy replied. "Said she comes on strong because she's got all that pent-up energy with no place for it to go, so she wraps it 'round the family."

"Well, she's sure made it clear over the years that she doesn't mind stepping on other people's feelings. She was mighty lucky to have someone like your grandfather. And your mother, too. Although she never really appreciated your mother like she should. Why, I'll never forget the way your mother brightened up that house when she came to live with them. Big Buck was like a little kid. She was like a ray of sunshine. Just the sight of her warmed him up all over. Even after she was grown, she still had that effect on him. Why, when she'd walk into the shop, he'd perk up like it was Christmas morning."

When Mac finished talking, a somber silence seemed to envelop the room, punctured only by the steady snipping of his scissors as the meaning of his words sunk in.

"Came to live with them?" the boy repeated, confused.

After a long silence, the barber feebly replied, "Why...yeah...sure...you know what I mean."

"No, Mac. What do you mean?"

The barber stopped cutting, his hands frozen awkwardly in the air holding his scissors and comb. "Well, you know...about your mother being adopted. Well, not really adopted...it all was in the family."

Little Buck felt a nausea rising from his stomach up through his chest until it seemed to lodge in his throat, cutting off his breath and nearly choking him. "In...the family?" his voice trailed off as he tried to swallow.

"Now wait a minute, I'm not telling you something you don't already know...about your mother being adopted, am I?"

"Course not. Course I knew," he mumbled weakly. "It's...it's just that they never talk about it much. How come you know about it?"

"How come I know about it?" the barber laughed. "Why, I was there, boy, when they brought your mother home."

"After she was born, you mean?"

"Heavens, no. She must have been around five. Right after her real mother, Mrs. Hart's sister, died. Why, Buck wouldn't let her out of his sight; he insisted on carrying her around in his arms, even though she really was too big for that. It was like she satisfied a craving in his life that he didn't even know he had until she showed up. Why, the two of them became inseparable. He loved your mother more than most fathers love their own children. To tell the truth, I always figured that it made Mrs. Hart a little jealous. Even though your mother was her own flesh and blood—her niece, actually—there was never any doubt about who she was closest to. Yes sir, Buck treated Mercy better than if she'd been his own daughter!"

As Mac removed the candy-striped sheet, shook some talcum powder on a soft-bristled brush, and dusted Little Buck's neck, he paused, smiling, "Yes sir, and he loved you, boy, more than if you was his own grandson!"

Sitting numbly in the barber's chair, dazed by the revelation, Little Buck clenched his jaw, trying to hold back his tears.

"Okay, boy. We're all done. What are you waiting for?" The barber cranked down the chair, grinning as he spun the boy around. "How's it look?" he pointed his scissors toward the mirrors on the wall.

The entire room seemed to be dizzily spinning as Little Buck stumbled out of the chair. "Looks good," he mumbled, clamping his chin against his chest to hide his face as he fumbled in his pocket for his money.

"Say, maybe you'd like to shine shoes for me on Saturdays. What do you say?"

Still fighting back tears, Little Buck slapped two quarters on the stand beside the cash register and choked out, "Maybe," as he ran out of the shop, leaving the door open behind him.

"What's wrong, boy?" the barber called after him.

Tears streamed down Little Buck's cheeks as he ran toward home, oblivious to everything around him except for the terrible tingling sensation wracking his body, the awful revelation that could not be true.

"He is my grandfather...he is...he is...," the boy repeated to the cadence of his pounding feet as he turned onto Oak Avenue and frantically raced for home.

Bursting through the side door and up the steps to the kitchen where his mother and grandmother were canning sauerkraut, the boy screamed hysterically, "Mac says that Big Buck isn't my real grandfather! Mac says..."

"Oh, Little Buck," his mother cried out, rushing to throw her arms around him, squeezing him as he sobbed uncontrollably on her shoulder.

"The bastard!" his grandmother hissed through clenched teeth, falling back against the sink as if she had been stricken.

"Well, is it true?" the boy looked pleadingly from his mother to his grandmother.

"Let's sit down in the living room and talk it out," his mother whispered, leading the bewildered little boy by the hand, as his tight-lipped grandmother followed imperiously.

"We were going to tell you when you were older," his mother began, sitting close to him on the couch, patting his hand. "It's too bad you had to hear it this way, but you shouldn't make more out of it than it is. It was all in the family...not like I was adopted out of some orphanage. Nan's actually my aunt. When my mother, Elizabeth, died, there were two little children who had to be cared for. My father, who was a superintendent at the Carnegie Works below Pittsburgh, couldn't look after my little brother and me."

"You mean he didn't want to," Nan scoffed.

"Well, for whatever reason, Nan and Big Buck were willing to take me in, to give me a home—a wonderful home—to treat me like their own daughter. So, they became my parents, more real to me than my original parents whom I could only vaguely recall."

"But...but your real father was still alive...my real grandfather."

Glancing at Nan, the boy's mother hesitantly replied, "Well, everyone seemed to agree that if I was going to be adopted by Nan and Big Buck, it wouldn't be good for me to have my real father coming in and out of my life. So, I guess that was a condition...," she shrugged and then hurriedly added, "for my own good, for their adopting me."

"But didn't he want to see you? He was your real father. He was my real grandfather. Didn't he want to see me?"

"He didn't care about anyone but himself, and strutting around lording his position over everyone," Nan sneered.

"Now, Mother," Mercy shook her head, frowning, "that's not fair. Anyway, he died before you were born, Little Buck. That's why we didn't think it was necessary to tell you until you were older. I know this comes as a great shock, and it's hard for you to understand, but the important thing for you to remember is that Nan and Big Buck created a wonderful, secure life for me...and for you, too. They're my real parents, and they're your real grandparents, too. Our biological relationship doesn't mean anything. It's the love and life which they've given us that counts."

"And the sacrifices we made for your mother and you," the boy's grandmother added softly, trying to smile. "And we never accepted a thing from that man! Even during the Depression when he tried to buy his way in here, we never took one cent from him!" Victoria Hart added proudly, unable even to speak the name of her dead sister's despised husband.

"But this means Big Buck and I aren't even related," the boy's words came between his muffled sobs, buried in his mother's arms.

"Now what would Big Buck think if he heard you saying that?" the boy's mother gently jostled him. "Why, a lifetime of love counts for a lot more than just having the same blood."

"How come we're both left-handed?"

"Well, that's something that really tickled Big Buck. You can't imagine how happy it made him. Who knows, maybe it was God's way of making you two alike."

"And you and I have the same widow's peak, Little Buck. That certainly shows that you're in the family," his grandmother smoothed back her glistening white hair.

"Why don't we have the tapioca pudding I was saving for dinner," his mother smiled, pushing back his hair to display his widow's peak.

Tears still streamed down Little Buck's cheeks as he pulled himself away, sniffling, "I don't feel like eating. I'm going back to bed," he said dejectedly as he started for the stairs.

"Your Dad should be home from Redstone soon," his mother called after him. "Maybe the two of you can go to the high school football game this afternoon."

Pretending not to hear her, Little Buck slowly climbed the stairs, suddenly too tired to lift one foot in front of the other. He was bewildered, unable to cope with the stunning revelation. He felt numb and dead inside, the way he had felt right after Big Buck's death. Falling into his bed, he pulled the pillow over his head and began sobbing again.

First, they take Big Buck away from me, and now, they take away our even being related, he thought. This just can't be...it's too awful to be true. This means I'm not even related to Rip or Emily. Wait 'til the other boys find out. All that stuff about Rip being my cousin...about me maybe being as good as him. No wonder I'm no good. We're not even related.

Little Buck cried himself to sleep and did not awaken until early afternoon when his father gently nudged him.

Chapter Eleven

Heartache

"How come you didn't tell me Mom was adopted...that Big Buck wasn't my real grandfather?" the boy asked, blinking open his eyes.

"Nan was dead set against it, kiddo," his father replied. "And you've got to see her side of it. At first, you were too young to understand, and then, when Big Buck died, she was afraid it would hurt you too much to know the truth. Anyway, it's not that big a deal. It was all in the family. She's really your great aunt."

"But this means I'm not even related to Big Buck, or to any of the Harts."

"You're a Helwig, boy. You've got plenty to be proud of on our side of the family. It was our ancestors that helped settle these parts long before the Harts ever thought about America or Pennsylvania. Why, it was your kin that came over the Alleghenies to fight the Indians, clear the land, and turn the wilderness into civilization. Your fifth great-grandfather, Michael Kepple Helwig, was Colonel Boquet's chief scout; he stood with him at the Battle of Bushy Run in 1763. And his son, Nicholas—your fourth great-grandfather— stood with Washington at the Battle of Germantown, where he got his eye shot out. He collected $9 a month disability pension, a large sum back then, until the day he died in 1819. Why, you and I qualify to belong to the American Sons of the Revolution. That's something the Harts can't claim!"

"How come we never joined?"

"Oh, your Granddad Helwig belonged. Went to the conventions and everything. Course, times have been hard on us lately. But someday...someday we'll have the money to step right out with the best of them. If it wasn't for the damned Depression, we'd be on easy street right now. Your Granddad Helwig was on his way to becoming one of the wealthiest men in this valley: first, the general store, then the real estate, the feed mill, the insurance business, the opera house, the savings and loan; then, between 1929 and 1932 it all went down the drain...wiped out, along with lots of other good men. Just because I've made a mess of my life is no reason for you not to be proud of the Helwig name. Someday you'll make something of yourself. You'll pick up where your Granddad Helwig left off. You're a lot like him, kiddo."

Little Buck shrugged as he slid out of bed, thinking: Maybe, but it's Big Buck that I want to be like. It's Big Buck that I'll never be able to see again. It's Big Buck who could explain all this to me and make it right.

Rejecting his father's offer of the football game, he walked softly into the kitchen, stuffed three bananas and a jar of peanut butter inside his shirt, and returned to his room. Peeling and quartering each banana with his penknife, he then plastered peanut butter on the inner sides and made two banana sandwiches. Uncharacteristically, he slowly savored each bite of his special treat as he sat cross-legged on his bed, staring out the window at the buckeye trees. The prickly green hulls of the buckeyes were beginning to turn a speckled brown. Surely they would start dropping soon. But what difference did it make, he sighed. Now he had three grandfathers, yet he had no grandfathers. He probably was the only boy in town who would go through life without ever knowing any of his grandfathers. Big Buck had been the most important person in his life, and suddenly, not only was he dead, he wasn't even his grandfather. He felt so empty and rejected, so alone and deceived.

He remembered how he and Big Buck had caught baseball nearly every summer evening in the alley behind their house; how he had swelled with pride when someone walked by, almost always commenting, "Looks like we got two lefties at work," or, "Chip off the old block," or, "Making a first baseman out of that grandson of yours, Buck?"

Maybe I'm not really left-handed, he thought. Maybe they just taught me to write and throw that way to please Big Buck. He reached into the basket near his bed, rooted around until he found a baseball, and then stood in front of the mirror practicing a throwing motion with his right hand. "Naw, it feels too awkward," he shook his head, tossing the ball back into the basket. "I'm left-handed. Wish I could have seen Big Buck's face when he first discovered it," the boy whispered to himself, smiling.

He spent the rest of the afternoon staring glumly through the window. When his chums came running and shouting down the street, apparently returning from another Steel Valley victory, he slid behind the curtain out of view. He couldn't face them. How was he ever going to tell them that Big Buck wasn't his real grandfather? Everyone always had made such a big deal about him being a carbon copy of his grandfather. But wouldn't their parents have known? Most of the families had come to town around the same time; most of his friends' grandparents had lived in the neighborhood since his mother had been a little girl. They surely knew she was adopted. Wouldn't they tell their grandsons? Nan told him all the gossip: About the love-babies, and old man Schmidt's sister, and how Shrimpy Cox's grandmother got put away. Everyone probably knew the story. He probably was the only person in town who didn't know that Big Buck wasn't his real grandfather. What a sneaky, dirty trick! They had made such a fool of him!

Throwing himself back onto his bed, he lay there clutching his pillow until he heard his mother's voice calling him for dinner. Since Big Buck's death, Nan had insisted that he sit at the head of the dining room table, in Big Buck's chair. Each evening as he had climbed up into the polished maple armchair—only he and his grandmother at the other end of the table had arms on their chairs—knowing that he was in Big Buck's chair, this had helped ease the pain, and had helped him feel connected to his grandfather. But now, he couldn't bring himself to go near the special chair. The very thought of sitting in it, of even touching it, was a sacrilege, a violation of Big Buck's memory, a desecration of a hallowed fixture in their home. For he was an impostor, neither flesh nor blood of the man he worshipped.

"Sit down, Little Buck, your dinner's getting cold," his grandmother commanded. "And don't gobble down your food."

Lugging a straight-backed chair from the corner of the room to beside his mother, he slid up on it and shifted his place setting in front of him.

"Now what's that all about?" his grandmother asked.

"I'm not sitting there anymore."

"That's your place, now that Big Buck's gone."

"No it isn't."

"Allan, you better straighten out that son of yours," Nan said, glaring at her son-in-law.

"Come on, boy, there's no cause for you to act like this," his father said.

"Big Buck would really be hurt if he thought you didn't want to sit in his chair," his mother coaxed.

"No!"

"Allan, you better take this boy in hand!" Nan said.

"Oh, let him be, Mother," Mercy said, reaching over and squeezing her son's hand. "He's been through a lot today."

After another squabble about Little Buck's refusal to say the blessing and its eventual recitation by his father, the family ate their dinner silently, with Victoria Hart sighing before each bite, while the boy's mother smiled at him pleadingly as he picked at his food. Only the boy's father enjoyed his dinner, piling his plate with a second helping of meatloaf, green beans, and mashed potatoes, the whole concoction smothered in thick gravy.

Midway through the dinner, Little Buck spoke to his mother.

"This morning you said you had a little brother. What happened to him?"

Hesitating, the boy's mother looked at his grandmother, who snapped, disgustedly tossing her napkin on the table, "You might as well tell him everything."

"Well, you remember Lawrence, who came to visit us from the Navy last month?"

"Sure."

"Well, he's my brother. Two years younger than I."

"Where's he been all this time? Who raised him?"

A long and awkward silence filled the dimly lit dining room. The hand-painted china, sterling silver utensils, lace tablecloth, and oil paintings seemed obscenely out of place as the boy's mother choked out her faint reply. "In an orphanage."

"An orphanage? You mean nobody wanted him?"

"That wasn't it at all," his grandmother stiffened. "There was a lot more to it than meets the eye."

"Like what?" the boy asked, incredulously.

"Well, for one thing, my sister, Mary, did take him in. She tried to raise him with her own children, but he was a bad boy, totally uncontrollable."

"He was only four years old," the boy's mother murmured, plaintively.

"Now you stay out of this, Mercy. Mary tried. We all tried to do our share. Goodness knows, Buck and I made sacrifices a plenty for you...and this boy...and Allan, too. If Allan had been a better provider we wouldn't be in the fix we're in today!"

"I thought you said my real grandfather was a superintendent in one of the Carnegie mills. He must have been well-off. Didn't he want his children? Didn't he want his own son?"

"You might as well know the truth, Joseph," Nan snorted. "He was no damn good! He was more inter- ested in gambling and drinking and catting around."

"Oh, Mother, that's not fair," Mercy pleaded.

"Then how'd he keep his job?" Little Buck asked.

"God only knows," Nan hissed.

"Mother, not in front of the boy."

"Well, certain things need to be brought out in the open. And I'm not going to sit here and be put on the defensive for what happened to your brother. I've done my share. More than my share!"

"You...you mean they just sent him away? To an orphanage? When you had all these rooms here?" Little Buck's face wrinkled in dismay.

"Pinned his name on his coat, handed him over to the conductor, and we stood there on the platform watching as the train pulled away," Little Buck's mother sniffled. "He was five and I was seven. It's a sight that'll be with me to my dying day."

"It's easy for you to sit there now, saying this, Mercy, but Buck and I were the ones who had the re- sponsibility and who had to worry about raising you."

"I know, Mother, and I'm grateful. Truly, I am. It's just that it seemed so awful to send that little boy away. Especially when Dad said that he could stay. I know you did what you thought was right, but I guess I'll never get over what was done to Larry."

"Well, I've just about had enough of this!" Victoria Hart pushed herself away from the table, strode haughtily into the living room, carefully adjusted her dress as she lay down upon the couch, and closed her eyes, extending her one arm straight up in the air.

As Little Buck and his mother washed the dishes that evening, he asked, "What's Larry's last name? What was your real name?"

"Campbell," his mother answered, softly.

"Campbell? That's not a German name!"

"My real father's name was Andrew Campbell. He was Scotch-Irish."

"Then I'm not even German." Little Buck's eyes darted pitifully from his mother to his father as tears welled up in them. Flinging his dishcloth on the sink, he ran out of the room and upstairs to his bedroom, with his mother calling after him, "But you're three-quarters German."

Slamming his bedroom door behind him, he crawled into the corner of his clothes closet, pulling the door shut. His chapped lips quivered and stung from the salty tears trickling down across them as he hunched into the far corner of the darkened closet. From out of his nearby shoeshine box wafted the smell of his old polish rags, reminding him of those glorious, gone-forever days, recalling how sometimes on busy Saturdays, at Big Buck's signal, he would slow down a shine, or apply an extra coat of polish, so his grandfather could gulp down a sandwich and a few sips of coffee before Little Buck released his customer from the chair.

"Big Buck knew all along we weren't even related, and he never told me," the boy spoke aloud, squeezing his arms around his knees until his wrists ached. "How could he have done that to me? Why would he waste his time with a little kid who he wasn't even related to...who wasn't even German?"

Several minutes passed as he sat doubled over in the closet, sniffling dejectedly, trying to fathom the maze of disjointed, jumbled feelings ricocheting through his body like frightened birds trapped inside a room, bouncing off closed windows, not knowing what to do.

A crease of light suddenly penetrated his warm, black world, and then splashed throughout his closet, blinding and exposing him as the closet door was opened. His father lifted him out of the closet onto the bed, where his mother helped him into his pajamas. Tucking him in bed, his mother spoke slowly and softly, yet more firmly than he had ever heard. "What you've learned today, son, has come as quite a shock. And we're sorry about the way you had to hear it. But it would be terrible if you let it affect the way you feel about Big Buck. Terrible for you, and terrible for Big Buck, too. Just because he's not here in person anymore doesn't mean his spirit isn't with us. You believe that, don't you?"

"I suppose so," Little Buck shrugged, rubbing a tear from his eye as he shivered, sliding more deeply beneath the covers. His spacious bedroom window rattled as a gust of wind swept through the buckeye trees and over the porch roof. The pale yellow flicker of the streetlight behind one of the trees seemed to bob about, caught in a crosscurrent of howling winds swooping through their valley beneath a cold, black, starless sky.

"You've got to try to understand how important, how special, you and I were to Big Buck, and to Nan, too. When they discovered they couldn't have any children of their own, it left a terrible emptiness in their lives, a gnawing ache they couldn't ease. They had this wonderful, big house, and no one to fill it; all their love and no one to share it with, or to give it to. Then, when my mother died, all that suddenly changed. A tragedy turned into a blessing. I became the daughter they never had, and what a blessing it was for me, too! Then you came along and were the son that Big

Buck never had. The joy you brought him is some-thing you'll never fully know." Little Buck's mother smiled, misty-eyed, as she pushed a lock of his soft blond hair back across his forehead.

"And when times got tough, we were mighty lucky they wanted to take us in," Little Buck's father added, "...and that Big Buck was such an extraordinary, good-hearted man. He never once gave me the feeling that he was trying to take my place, or lord his position over me. I was just happy that you could have so many people loving you. Especially after the war started and I had to be away so much."

"But what about Nan? She never liked us being here."

"That's where you're way off base, kiddo. She could do without me being around, that's for sure," the boy's father laughed, "but as far as she's concerned...why, the sun rises and sets on you."

"That's a fact," Little Buck's mother reassured him. "You've got to understand your grandmother. She'd gladly lay down her life for you. It's just that she's got all that vitality and ambition and talent, and no place to let it out except here in the home, with the family."

"So she spends it trying to make the house per-fect, then trying to make herself perfect, then trying to make the rest of us perfect, too," the boy's father shook his head. "She wants for you all the things that she couldn't have for herself. So, she's pinned all her hopes on you. And, of course, that's exactly how Big Buck felt, too. Now, how can you turn your back on him just because he doesn't happen to be your bio-logical grandfather? Why, he's more real than either of your real grandfathers. Why, you were the most important thing in his life."

"It would break his heart if he thought you were going to love him any less because of this," Little Buck's mother said, patting his hand. "You think about it, and get a good night's sleep," she leaned over and kissed him.

Tousling his hair, his father kissed him on the forehead and whispered as he flicked out the light, "Tomorrow's Sunday morning, kiddo...Dutch Cake and coffee-soup time."

Lying in the dark, Little Buck listened to the wind howling through the buckeye trees, rattling his window, causing the streetlight to sway and flicker. He didn't know what to think. A few large drops of rain splattered against his window; a bolt of lightning flashed behind the hillside, above the old abandoned coal mine. A few seconds later, a clap of thunder shook the sky, and the rain came pelting down upon the tin porch roof beneath his window. Emotionally exhausted from the day's events, he fell into a deep sleep.

Chapter Twelve

Dreams Can Come True

A little before dawn, he was awakened by the rat-a-tat-tat rhythm of buckeyes bouncing on the porch roof beside his bedroom window. The rain had stopped, but the branches of the buckeye trees were still swaying in the wind. A deluge of buckeyes hailed down upon the roof, clogging the gutters and rainspouts, spilling over the edge and bouncing off the sidewalk, or rolling underneath the ivy beneath the buckeye trees.

Opening his eyes wide, instantly he knew the meaning of the sounds. Taking a deep, satisfying sigh, he grinned and interlocked his hands behind his head, stretching every muscle in his body. Lying perfectly still, he listened to the rhythmic patter upon the roof, trying to visualize the size of his harvest, wondering if his double buckeyes would be hard to find.

Several minutes later, the first gray light of dawn glimmered in the sky behind the old abandoned coal mine. The clang of hammered steel sounded faintly in the distance. The smell of fresh-brewed coffee curled up the stairs, and a crack of light shone brightly beneath his bedroom door. No need rush until I can see, he told himself, studying the slowly expanding strip of gray rising in the eastern sky behind the hill, savoring the long awaited moments that lay ahead. The first thing he would do was throw away last year's moldy double buckeyes, even before beginning his search for new ones. That was Big Buck's style. "We're starting fresh, kiddo," he had always said. "Don't be afraid to put what's past behind you. Stake everything you've got on the future. Then, you'll work twice as hard to make it come true."

A slim, pink glow shimmered behind the hilltop as puffs of white appeared across the cold, gray sky. The wind calmed into a breeze, and in the new day's light, Little Buck could see the spent raindrops glistening on the shiny horse chestnut leaves. Then his eyes lit upon the porch roof, littered with twigs and leaves and buckeye hulls. Some of the buckeyes had burst from their prickly hulls upon impact and had rolled into the gutters. It was nearly impossible to match double buckeyes once they had been separated from their shell. From his window, he could see that a few of the loose buckeyes had split open. They would be totally worthless—no good for miniature pipes, nor for baseball card or marble swaps. But, most of the buckeyes were still intact in their hulls. Hundreds were on the porch, alone. Thousands had to be buried in the ivy beneath the trees. It would be his biggest harvest ever. Ten buckeyes for a marble, fifty for a glassy shooter, and a hundred for a steely—those would be his opening offers. As for the baseball cards, well, it depended. Even though he already had four Gerhig's, he'd given a whole bag of buckeyes for another. But, of course, he wouldn't tell that to any of his chums, unless it was his final offer.

He considered getting dressed and eating breakfast, maybe even having coffee soup and Dutch Cake with his father. After breakfast he could get the grocery bags his mother had been saving for him and begin his harvest on the porch roof. All before Sunday school. He would have to hurry.

Then, he remembered his grandmother's fuss and his mother's fear each time he had crawled onto the porch roof. Every year his grandmother had forbidden it, but Big Buck had always interceded, "Come on, Victoria, that roof's not steep. It's only fifteen feet above the ground. The boy climbs our trees like a monkey. You're going to turn him into a sissy. Let him be. Go ahead, kiddo, get your buckeyes."

Looking through his bedroom window at his anticipated harvest, the boy spoke aloud, "What do you think, Big Buck? Best I slip out now, before Nan can get too riled." Then he felt the pang of the previous day's disclosure. Tears welled up in his eyes and his lower lip quivered as he wrote his initials, J H H, in the condensation on the window. He drew a line through his middle initial, then wiped it clean with his sleeve, blew his breath on the spot to fog it over again, and then re-wrote a large H between his smaller first and last initials. Pressing his nose against the glass, he closed one eye and sighted through the uprights of the large H, spotting a fallen branch laden with clusters of buckeyes dangling precariously from a rain spout. Peering at it, he was certain that a bulging hull in the center of the branch contained a set of double buckeyes.

Pushing up his window, he climbed onto the porch roof, crawling gingerly on all fours across the wet, leaf-covered roof to the edge. Bracing one foot on the rain gutter, he stretched his arm to snatch the branch. He could feel his heart pounding as the rain gutter shifted. "Gotcha!" he exclaimed, pulling the branch onto the porch as he scrambled backward toward his window. Once inside, he was astonished to discover that the prize hull appeared to have a duplicate hanging next to it on the other side of the branch. He snapped the two extraordinary hulls off their stems and set the branch back on the roof outside his window.

Taking a penknife from his dresser, he made a light surgical cut around the first hull, and then with his thumb and forefingers gently popped it open. Two magnificent shining buckeyes rested, side by side, in the creamy inner skin of the buckeye shell. Double buckeyes! The largest, shiniest, most perfectly matched pair he had ever seen! Then he repeated his procedure on the second hull. It popped open, and in his hands he held another set of double buckeyes, exactly like the first. He was so surprised by his discovery, that for a moment he didn't trust his own judgment. Taking both sets out of their shells, he held a set in each hand, comparing them, jiggling them into different positions for further examination.

He carefully laid the first pair in one corner of his dresser and the second pair in the other corner beneath the mirror. Suddenly realizing that he had not yet disposed of the two old sets of double buckeyes, he scooped them out of his dresser drawer, turned toward his open window, and hurled them through it, shouting out a joyous "Yahoo!"

"What's wrong?" his grandmother came bolting through his bedroom door, still in her nightgown and robe.

"Nothing," he said, standing in front of his dresser. "Buckeyes have finally starting falling. That's all," he motioned toward the trees.

"Please shut that window, Little Buck. You'd think you were born in a barn," she spoke softly, smiling at him. "And please don't be climbing out on that roof. Why don't you get yourself dressed for church, and let's have breakfast together," she nodded, encouragingly.

"Yes, ma'am," he said, surprised by her display of affection. The harvest can wait until this afternoon, he thought, holding up to the mirror his two new sets of buckeyes, wondering if there might be some way to tell scientifically if they really were exact duplicates. To the naked eye there could be no question. Hurriedly washing his face and combing his hair, he got into his white shirt with clip-on necktie and tweed suit. Inserting the two new sets of double buckeyes deep into his pants' pockets, he then leaped down the stairs, two at a time, ran into the kitchen, and threw himself up onto his chair, grinning.

"What's got you so perked up, kiddo?" his father asked as he poured a cup of coffee for the boy and pushed the toast, cream and sugar toward him. When his grandmother smiled and nodded her approval, he hurriedly broke a piece of toast into his coffee and added cream and sugar. As he ate his coffee soup, his father patted his arm, and for the first time since his grandfather's death he felt warm and good inside. He then wolfed down a slab of Dutch Cake plastered with butter, dunking it down to his second knuckles without a single objection from anyone.

Sometimes it pays to let people know your sad, to let them see your feelings, he thought. But Rip always said, "Never let them know your hurting. Just suck it up and keep on going." What would Big Buck say, the boy wondered. He'd tell me, "Just be yourself, and everything will work out all right." That would be his style.

"Maybe you'd like to gather some buckeyes on the sidewalk while your father and I finish dressing for church," his mother suggested.

"Afternoon's time enough for that. I'll just wait for you in the living room," Little Buck replied, thinking: Best I not be messing with any other buckeyes now; they might dilute the power of the two perfect sets I've found—the two perfect sets that found me. Best I get the feel of them, and let them start to work their charm, he thought, tightly grasping each set in a hand stuffed into each pants' pocket.

On their way to church, he walked between his parents, keeping his hands in his pockets to rub his buckeyes, trying to concentrate on their magic and how touching them, somehow, made him feel the presence of his grandfather.

Throughout Sunday school, he was oblivious to Rip's lesson and to the friendly nudges of his chums, trying instead to understand the meaning of the past two days, trying to make some sense out of all that had happened, trying to decide what he should believe—what he should feel—about the revelation that Big Buck wasn't his real grandfather. How should he handle it? What should he say? His mind burned with the intensity of his questions. His entire body seemed aflame. Yet, he couldn't find the answer. It was as though he were groping his way through a heavy smog, a dank oppressiveness, knowing that a golden sun and pure sweet air lie waiting for him somewhere, yet unable to find his direction, not knowing which way to turn. Overhead, he heard the church bell slowly ringing, not the solid vibrant call that he and Big Buck could coax from it, but a weak and doleful tolling.

He climbed up the back stairs to the sanctuary to avoid his friends and the ushers who might ask his help. Sliding into the end seat of their pew, next to his mother, he forced a smile and sat down. His cousin, Emily, got up from her seat a few rows behind him and slipped into their row on the other side of his mother. Leaning across, she patted his knee and whispered, "Got some fresh apple cider and cinnamon sticks. Why don't you come over after supper and we'll light a fire and heat some up?"

Smiling at her, he nodded his agreement. No matter how busy she was, Emily always took time for him. And now, it was as though she sensed his special need for her affection. Yes, Little Buck decided, Emily had an uncanny sixth sense—"intuition" was what she called it. And he could develop it, too, she had assured him, if he paid close attention to other peoples' words, and tone of voice, and facial expressions, and body language. "Try to feel the subtle nuances," she had counseled, "and you'll begin to appreciate how they're thinking. And once you know that, you'll know how to persuade them to your point of view."

She's done it again, Little Buck smiled to himself. Somehow, she's figured out that today I need an awful lot of loving.

A few minutes later, Rip slid into the seat beside the boy, nudging him playfully. Grinning at his famous cousin, Little Buck squirmed in the hard church pew. Elbowing him again, Rip leaned over, whispering, "Coach tells me you're doing good; says you'll make a halfback; says you got my speed."

Shrugging uncomfortably, the boy thought: Maybe Rip doesn't know I'm not his real cousin. But surely someone's going to tell him, now that it's out. His mother had to poke him to stand when the congregation rose at the preacher's call to worship, and he heard none of the announcements nor the Scripture lesson. When they rose to sing a hymn, he held his half of the hymnal with Rip, while Emily and his mother shared. But he didn't even bother to read the words. Only when his father winked at him from the choir loft did he grin a little.

The part of the service he dreaded most was fast approaching. When the preacher called for the offering, the undertaker and Mr. Clay strode forward to get the plates. It took the president of the bank to replace Big Buck, the boy thought, observing the dullness of the banker's shoes as he approached their pew.

While the ushers stood in the back of the church with their full collection plates, the choir rose to sing a hymn. Once again, Little Buck's father was the soloist, stepping to the front of the choir loft in his newly pressed black robe, his clear tenor voice rising above the resonating pipe organ, reverberating past the stained glass windows, filling the sanctuary and balcony above.

Squeezing his eyes tightly shut, Little Buck clutched his two new sets of double buckeyes in his hands, and let his father's voice penetrate his soul, cleansing, energizing, yet calming him. He could feel the warm touch of his mother's arm on his left, and the strength of his cousin's muscles on the other side. Without opening his eyes, he knew his mother's face would be aglow with happiness, gazing serenely at her husband. And Emily probably would be restlessly fingering her gold-plated rose pin, the one he had saved up to buy for her last Christmas. Taking a deep, slow breath through his nostrils, he could almost smell Nan's chicken giblets cooking, see her moving resolutely between the dining room and kitchen, basting the chicken with her savory homemade gravy, setting out her hand-painted china plates, putting in the center of the table her china fruit bowl with the painted cherries on it—the one that she had promised would belong to him someday. The candles in their polished silver holders would soon be lit, and the Victrola would be cranked for Strauss waltzes or a Chopin polonaise. Their succulent Sunday dinner—far superior to anything his friends had ever tasted—would be placed upon the table, in surroundings fit even for old Andy Carnegie, himself.

As the anthem ended and the doxology rang from the fullness of the pipe organ, the congregation rose to join the choir in singing. Little Buck knew that the ushers would begin their measured steps down the aisle to arrive in front of the preacher precisely as the last word was sung. And in his mind's eye in the moments that followed, he saw his grandfather, Big Buck, carrying the collection plate down the aisle, his starched white collar and French cuffs extending exactly one inch beyond his pin-striped suit. He was certain that he detected the slightest tug on his elbow as the usher passed his pew, and in that instant he felt a warm, tingling sensation flowing through his body. His body seemed to be floating weightlessly, up into a dream world that, yet, was real. Cautiously opening his eyes, he saw as through a gentle haze the two ushers standing with their backs to him. Could it be...could it possibly be? The usher on the right was Big Buck! It *was* his grandfather!

As the preacher entoned his blessing upon the offering, the little boy leaned forward and whispered in the direction of the usher on the right, "It's all right, Big Buck. I've finally found our double buckeyes. Everything's going to be okay."

Epilogue

After graduating with honors from Steel Valley High School where he captained the baseball team, attending the University of Pennsylvania on an academic scholarship, and then graduating from its law school, Joseph Hart Helwig—or Buck Helwig to his friends—eventually became a distinguished attorney and civic leader.

Thirty years to the day, after he had crawled out of his bedroom window onto the porch roof to retrieve his two new sets of double buckeyes, Joseph Hart Helwig was elected to the Congress of the United States from Pennsylvania's Twenty-sixth District.

Two months later, he was making his way across the Capitol grounds to the House chamber for his swearing in, a few minutes before noon on January 3, surrounded by his family, and followed by a bevy of well-wishers, reporters, and television cameras.

"Heard a rumor you're going to challenge one of the senior members of the delegation for his seat on the Ways and Means Committee," one of the reporters called out.

"Wouldn't think of it. That's not my style," the congressman-elect replied, nodding his head to accentuate his words, a trait that had become his trademark.

Suddenly, he stopped, noticing a cluster of stately horse chestnut trees in the southwest corner of the

Capitol grounds. "Excuse me for a moment," he said, pushing through the crowd to one of the trees. Kneeling down, his hands moved deftly among the brown hulls beneath the tree. Finally pausing, he seemed to be carefully fingering one of the hulls. Then, as he broke it open, two shiny buckeyes emerged.

With television cameras grinding, a reporter asked, "What in the world are you doing, Mr. Congressman?"

"You mean you haven't heard?" he squinted at the reporter, holding up the buckeyes. "Double buckeyes, double luck. And where I'm going, I'll need all the luck I can get," he laughed.

Then, he bent over again, resuming his search until he found a second pod. Breaking it open, two more shiny buckeyes fell into his hand.

"Who are they for?" another reporter asked.

Smiling wistfully as he put the buckeyes in his pocket, Congressman Joseph Hart Helwig replied, "For the greatest man I ever knew—Joseph Hart. My grandfather."

About the Author, and Why "Your" Dreams Can Still Come True

Although a work of fiction, *Double Buckeyes* is based in part on Bud Shuster's life growing up in a small town in the Monongahela valley of western Pennsylvania during the Great Depression and World War II. The shaving mug story really happened. Shortly after Bud Shuster's grandfather died, he did trudge through the snow on a cold winter night to deliver a hand-painted shaving mug to Congressman Samual A. Weiss. The mug had belonged to the congressman's father, Asa Weiss, a Jewish immigrant, who had died not knowing that his son, Sammy, would some day be elected to the Congress of the United States.

The brief encounter at the congressman's home, the witnessing of the congressman's extraordinary ability to help so many people through hard and dangerous times, made an indelible impact on 11-year-old Bud Shuster. For one shining instant, his little world—a worn-out fuliginous valley of dreary steel mills and frightened people—had been transmuted into a magical room where a single man possessed the ability to right the wrongs being inflicted upon good people all about him. Nearing his home, he stopped knee deep in snow and announced to the stars in the frigid winter sky, "Someday I'm going to be a congressman."

Nearly three decades later, he made his dream come true. But not without successes and failures, hard work and heartaches, doubts and detours, and the help and love of many along the way.

His earlier dream of becoming a major league baseball player quickly faded when he couldn't hit a curve ball or make the throw from center field to home. His hopes of becoming a lawyer as a logical path to Congress were dashed when he had to earn a living to make ends meet. But he never lost his dream.

Although growing up in hard times, in a home of modest means, he had the great gift of a loving family who believed in him. From their encouragement and example, he drew the strength to persevere, fondly recalling how his mother ran through his Latin vocabulary cards with him each morning as he gulped down his breakfast. Or of his father instilling in him the pride of their ancestors having been among the pioneer settlers of western Pennsylvania, of having fought the Indians, cleared the land and helped plant a new civilization on the western slopes of the Alleghenies.

He graduated with high honors from Glassport High School, earning his varsity letter on a championship basketball team, but hastening to describe himself as the poorest player on the team. Winning an academic scholarship to the University of Pittsburgh, he never forgot the severe tongue lashing he got from his high school principal on the day the principal informed him he had won the scholarship: "Shuster, I'm probably going to regret recommending you for this scholarship. You're going to go down there, thinking you can slide through without studying, and end up flunking out. I will have made a terrible mistake by not recommending a more deserving student. Don't you ever forget, at a big university like Pitt, it's survival of the fittest."

Thrilled with the opportunity to enter college rather than the gate of one of the steel mills in the valley, and burning with a mixture of shame and anger from the lecture he had just received from the very man who had made his opportunity possible, Bud Shuster resolved, with every fiber in his body, that he would prove his principal wrong. He not only would survive. He would excel to the very best of his ability.

His resolution began taking shape as he stood in the shadows of a flickering campfire at the University of Pittsburgh's freshman indoctrination week in the Allegheny mountains. The previous year's graduate, who had been named the "Outstanding Senior" of his class, was telling the new freshmen that the next four years could be the most important, most formative years of their lives. He explained how they could become "streetcar" students, returning to their homes after classes each day, or could become involved in campus life, getting full value for their education. He said that if you really dedicate yourself and organize each hour of the day, you can find the time to hit the books and learn as much outside the class as in. He had been captain of the Pitt debate team, president of the men's honor society, and several other organizations.

As Bud Shuster weighed the words of the outstanding graduate, and as he studied the faces of his new classmates and the dancing flames that removed the chill of an early September evening, he set his four-year goal: to be named the outstanding senior of his class. Never mind that as a product of a small mill town's public school system he would be competing with students from many of America's best private and public schools. Never mind that he had never even set foot inside that university, or any other before that very week. He decided on the spot, that, like the camp-fire speaker, he would become a college debater even though he had never even heard a debate, let alone participated in one. The very audacity of his dream exhilarated him.

When he received his grades on the first semester's transcript, he raced to Glassport High School, dashed into the principal's office, and upon confronting him, without a word, slapped his transcript on the counter in front of the principal—four A's and a B! He describes it as one of the most satisfying moments of his life, over which he and the principal had a good laugh many years later.

Along the way, during the summers and on weekends, to earn money for expenses and to help out at home, he worked as a gandy dancer on a railroad track gang, dug ditches, sold shoes, carried mail, washed cars, waited on tables, kept store for an Objibwe Indian tribe in the Canadian North Woods, operated a Kiddyland ride in an amusement park, and played the piano in a dance band which played for Polish weddings and in a roadhouse of allegedly ill-repute.

He took the advice not to become a "streetcar" student, organizing every hour of every day, immersing himself in his studies, and eventually becoming president of the senior honor society, the interfraternity council, and his beloved Sigma Chi fraternity. From that fraternity relationship, he developed his closest lifelong friendships. For over forty years, about a dozen of his fraternity brothers and their wives, who were their college sweethearts, have maintained their bonds of friendship. Although separated geographically, they get together several times each year. Annually, on the third weekend in June they gather at the Shuster farm, and on Sunday morning, they assemble in the black walnut grove beside the Juniata River which bounds the farm. There, in a circle, they conduct their church service, each person participating, Quaker style. The group includes an internationally renowned radiologist, several executives, two pastors, five educators, an attorney, a congressman, and their wives. They have shared in each other's joys and sorrows, sickness and health, throughout their lives. They are living proof that deep bonds of friendship developed in one's youth, if nourished, can profoundly enrich a person's life.

Four years after Bud Shuster entered Pitt, the boy who had never even heard a debate won the Grand National Debate Championship, and stood in silent awe as his name was engraved upon the university's campus walk—as he was named the outstanding senior of his class, a Phi Beta Kappa graduate of the university. The dream he had embraced around the freshman campfire had come true. He had converted that dream into a goal composed of many precise subgoals and had set out to achieve them. He discovered that the satisfactions one got from supposedly hard work made the work not hard at all. The efforts extracted very little sacrifice and produced enormous satisfactions. He learned that a dream is a goal you give your heart to; that a goal is a dream with muscle added.

To him it was a stunning revelation; it was as if he had discovered one of the world's great mysteries, had inadvertently stumbled upon a magic truth—that one can make something come true by believing it can come true; that belief can cause events to happen. In the years that followed, he saw that maxim occur time and time again. For him, it became as real as the laws of physics, yet not so simple or assured.

He learned that not all dreams come true, but more important, what is never dreamed can never be fulfilled. He learned that unfulfilled dreams have a way of branching into new possibilities; that even when a positive belief comes head to head with a stubborn, immovable reality, it finds new paths that lead to other opportunities, like a sunflower that blossoms by leaning toward the sun. Throughout his life he has never lost his sense of awe in the magic of belief, never quite understanding it, yet not doubting what he repeatedly experienced. And he witnessed those around him in America achieving many of their dreams, too.

After Pitt, Bud Shuster entered the Army as an officer and counter-intelligence agent. Marrying his high school sweetheart, Patricia Rommel, they have five children: Peg, Bill, Deb, Bob, and Gia. At last count, they are grandparents of eight: Bobby, Ali, Megan, Garrett, Emily, Gregory, Will, and Michael.

Following his military service, Bud Shuster went to work for UNIVAC, where he was involved in the installation of some of the early large scale computers in America, and the development of COBOL, the first English language software system. He became a vice president of RCA's computer division at the age of 33, and the chairman of a computer terminal company and a founder of a computer software company at 36, while earning his M.B.A. and Ph.D. at night.

His life has not been without its heartaches. His mother, through a series of progressive surgeries, had both her legs amputated. But she never lost her faith, and for thirteen years she wheeled herself to work each day, took her turn hosting her Sunday school class, and opened her heart to all who climbed her wheelchair ramp.

At the age of six, one of his children was diagnosed with acute leukemia, and he and his wife spent several heartwrenching days in the children's cancer ward at the National Institutes of Health with other grief-stricken parents. Finally, they were told their child had been misdiagnosed, and that she had another life-threatening illness that could be cured through surgery. It was an ordeal they never would forget, most especially the anguish of the other parents whose children could not be saved.

Years later, in a head-on collision, Bud Shuster's neck was broken while riding as a passenger in the front seat of a car. His seatbelt saved his life, but it took several operations for the surgeons to put his neck back together with mylar pins and a bone from his hip. Within a year, he was back running three miles a day and lifting weights, a lifetime fitness regimen that the doctors credit with helping to save his life.

After their old farmhouse burned to the ground, along with many prized family possessions, they gathered rough-cut stones from nearby abandoned old coke ovens and built Shuster Lodge on the same spot. As a legacy for future generations, they deeded it to their children, with an acre set aside for each grandchild. On one of the large stones beside the front door are the engraved words:

Dedicated to those who came before
who built so we might thrive

And high up right below the eaves of the side roof among the stones is a chiseled white stone Norman cross, the symbol of Bud Shuster's fraternity to which both his sons now belong, and where, at Penn State, one of his daughters was named the sweetheart of Sigma Chi. Even adversities provided opportunities to build anew and strengthen family traditions.

In 1972, never before having run for public office, he was elected to the U.S. Congress from the Ninth District in Central Pennsylvania. He is the only Pennsylvanian in history to have won both the Republican and Democratic congressional nominations eight times. He currently serves as chairman of the Transportation and Infrastructure Committee, the largest committee in the Congress, known as the "building" committee, with responsibility for all modes of transportation, including safety, from aviation to ocean shipping, as well as economic development, flood control and disaster relief. As a principal author of most of America's transportation and economic development legislation spanning the past two decades, his legislative passions have been improving transportation, saving lives, and creating jobs.

He also served as the ranking member of the Intelligence Committee, where he was deeply involved in America's battle against terrorism, communism, and illegal drugs.

While immersed in many legislative battles in Washington through the years, Bud Shuster deplores the increasingly bitter political atmosphere. But he continues to believe that the opportunity to help people and rebuild America far outweighs the slings and arrows of public life.

He previously served on the Budget Committee, the Education and Labor Committee, as chairman of the Republican Policy Committee, as a delegate to NATO's North Atlantic Assembly, and is a trustee of the Kennedy Center and the National Symphony Orchestra. He has been a delegate to six Republican National Conventions, and is the recipient of numerous awards, including an honorary Doctor of Laws degree from St. Francis College.

He is the author of the award-winning book, *Believing in America*, (published by Morrow, 1982; Berkley paperback, 1983) from which part of the story of his early life is retold here.

A former Pennsylvania interscholastic basketball referee, he is an avid runner, horseman, and hunter, as well as accomplished pianist who has performed with the Altoona Symphony Orchestra. When not in Washington, he resides on a farm in Bedford County, Pennsylvania, with his family.

Sitting on a shelf in his den is a hand-painted shaving mug, painted by his grandmother at the turn of the century. Rescued from his grandfather's old barber shop, it reminds him and his family, and all who care to see, that if one little boy's dream can come true in America, so can the dreams of many others.